FIVE MILES SOUTH OF TOWN

FIVE MILES SOUTH OF TOWN

Olga Berg

Palmetto Publishing Group
Charleston, SC

FIVE MILES SOUTH OF TOWN
Copyright © 2020 by Olga Berg

First Edition

Printed in the United States

ISBN-13: 9781641118026
ISBN-10: 1641118024

Cover Photos: (Top) John Stewart, (Bottom) Harlen Haughn

Thanks to:
Judy Dees - Editor
and Deborah Billingsley Photography

Other Books by Olga Berg

The Promise of a New Day

Dedication

To Those Who Knew Them

HARLEN HAUGHN

TABLE OF CONTENTS

FOREWORD

With a distance of twenty-two years between the first born and the last born, in this family of six children, gives the author a unique perspective in recording events that engulfed her family during their time on earth.

Being the last member of a family that goes back to the French Revolution on one side and William the Conqueror on the other side places the responsibility on her shoulders to either remain silent or pass on to future generations, the facts as they are known about our ancestors. This book is one of three that will trace their lives through records left behind of their deeds, failures and accomplishments for future generations to judge.

Thornton Wilder says: "All that we can know about those we have loved and lost, is that they would wish us to remember them with a more intensified realization of their reality. What is essential does not die but clarifies. The highest tribute to the dead is not grief but gratitude."

1

JOB DESCRIPTION
FOR COWBOYS

On a sunny, humid day in late summer, a wagon pulled by horses and loaded with hay stopped beneath the opening to the barn loft.

Standing waist deep in the fresh-cut fodder, three men whose long-sleeved shirts were wet with sweat - front and back - jabbed a pitchfork into the straw, lifted a sizeable load, then pitched it up and through the opening into the loft.

Two men inside the loft moved the sweet-smelling hay against the back wall, where it grew in height until the thrust of the loaded pitchfork could no longer reach its top.

When his father called, Harlen jumped down from the wagon and hurried to him. He observed the pained and stern expression on his face and guessed it was a serious matter that was to be discussed that caused his dad to walk all the way to the barn.

"Son," he said while leaning against the fence, "I want you to take the last group of cattle I bought and left at the Martin Place to the stockyards at West Plains. You won't go all the way into town as the stockyard is five miles south of town."

Harlen wondered at the timing - in the middle of mowing hay and stacking it in the barn loft for winter feed. He glanced back at the barn.

He thought also, about the dun colored gelding that had been brought to the farm just two days earlier from across the state line in Missouri by a man who said, "I bought the animal for my daughter and want it 'gentled' so she can ride it. She named it Star." He added, "I was told you could take the buck out of any horse," and he left the animal in Harlen's care.

Harlen had had little time to work with Star, but he left the horse in the barn lot with the other animals, and he seemed safe enough there.

"Well, Dad I..." The expression on his dad's face stopped him from saying anything more.

Joe's blue eyes hardened and wrinkles appeared on his forehead. Running his fingers through his thick black hair, he stared at Harlen. "Your brothers have gone out to California and you're the only one left at home to help me," he said. "You're eighteen years old. You're a man now. You've got to do this."

His voice grew louder and higher in pitch.

"Get a crew together. Then we'll make the final plans."

Joe turned away, looked across the fenced-in barn lot toward the house and rubbed his sore back. He limped a few steps then stopped. Without turning he said, "Pick your men. Six or eight 'ought to be enough. We'll talk some more later."

Harlen knew there was no use in arguing, but he called after his dad. "How long will this take? How many cattle?"

The words had just entered his thought pattern – had not settled in, for he was fighting the very thought of it.

Joe did not answer, for at that time, he didn't actually have an answer.

Again, he called after his dad, "When do you want me to start?"

Joe stopped, and this time he turned to face his son. "Well, there's fifty-six head I left at the Martin Place. Our neighbor John Baxter wants to join us in the drive with his fifteen head. Now, let's see," he paused, mentally adding up the number. "That makes seventy-one. There may be two or three little runty calves thrown in who were abandoned by their mothers."

As he laid out his plans, the stern expression on his face changed to a thoughtful one.

"I've got to talk to the neighbors about crossing their fields on the way to West Plains," he said. "Until my back gets better, I can't get up in the saddle, but we can go in the wagon. I want you to go with me."

That wasn't a command. It was a request. He simply could not make the trip himself for he was in too much pain. He needed his son's help.

Joe removed his hat, pulled a blue handkerchief from the pocket of his overalls, and wiped sweat off his face. He stuffed the handkerchief back in his pocket and gazed across the pasture seeing cows in the distance. Then looking toward the barn, he saw men's heads poking out of the loft looking at him.

"The drive should take no more than three days. Four at the most. I signed a contract with a man named Waymon Jenkins, from the sale barn, for delivery two Saturdays from now," he said. "If you keep the cattle moving, three nights and four days ought to be enough. We'll load the wagon with food and supplies. Skinner can drive it." He turned to leave. Then turning his head a little he said, "I'm going to the house now. I've got to sit down or maybe just lie down."

Harlen began to understood all this and said no more. He watched his dad walk slowly while holding on to the top railing with his right hand. Unable to stand straight, his body leaned a little to the left. Bending his knees to steady his steps, he followed the split rail fence row across the barn lot toward the house.

He noticed his dad's pantlegs were not tucked into his brown leather, knee-high, lace-up boots. Whether wearing overalls or a suit, the pant legs were always tucked in. Harlen suspected the soreness of his body prevented him from bending over.

Chickens squawked and scattered away from the fence, running and flapping their wings to escape his approach. One old hen flew too close to Crabby, the lone gander on the farm. True to his disposition he stuck out his neck, hissed through his open beak and ran after the hen with the intention of pecking her. Upon seeing and hearing the cantankerous gander, she flew to the top railing on the fence. Crabby hissed a few more times then turned and sauntered away.

It had been a week since he returned from a cattle buying trip where he bought fifty-six bovines and drove them some thirty miles to the Martin Place where he left them. His mule knew the way home, and upon arrival, it stopped in front of the house, but severe pain prevented Joe from getting out of the saddle.

Harlen and a couple of farm hands noticed his approach but were busy mending a portion of the fence that surrounded the barn lot which had been knocked down by two large bulls pushing and butting each other. After a moment or so, they became aware that he had made no effort to get off the mule and walked over to see why.

"Boys, help me down. I'm hurt," he said. "A half-grown yearling pushed me against a fence post then butted me a few times before I could get out of the way. I'm sore as the dickens."

Getting him off the animal and onto the ground was no easy job since Joe was in considerable pain and taller than those who had come to his aid. It took the three of them to help him up the six steps leading onto the veranda then into the sitting room and into his chair.

"Dad, how did you get the cattle here? Did you drive them by yourself?"

"No. I had help. The man I bought them from and his boys rode with me all the way."

Harlen's mother Laura rushed into the room. "Joe, what happened? How bad are you hurt?"

He led the way out of the room and headed toward the barn, knowing his dad would be well taken care of. Observing the empty wagon and glancing at the lowering sun, he unhitched the horses and led them the short distance to the pond.

Grasshoppers took to the air as the tall grass and weeds were disturbed with each step by the man and his animals. With lowered heads, the gentle plow horses drank the cool, still water. A frog jumped into the pond followed by another a few feet away. Ripples slowly crossed the water and broke on the animal's noses.

Harlen stood patiently, deep in thought. A whip-poor-will started his lengthy call and a breeze cooled his shirt, wet from perspiration, which stuck to his chest and back. The men who had helped unload the hay walked toward the pond, stirring up more grasshoppers and other buzzing and flying insects.

"Mr. Haughn looks pretty stove up," Price said as he approached the pond bank. The others mumbled in agreement.

Harlen shook his head and stared into the murky water. "Yeah. I guess he's pretty sore. He wants six or eight of us, maybe nine counting me, to take a herd of cattle to a stockyard just south of West Plains, Missouri."

"How many?" Price asked.

"Seventy-one. Maybe a few extra calves."

"That'll be a trail drive for sure. Eight men? That'll be enough. When do we start?"

"I don't know the exact day, but I expect maybe a couple of weeks from now," Harlen replied.

Trailing a herd of cattle forty miles and being responsible for its success was a big job for an eighteen-year old. He wasn't looking forward to any part of it. He was happiest riding Old Don across the pastures, seeing to the farm work and bringing in the crops.

The men swatted at bugs which swarmed in the early evening in the hot, damp weather. They stood silently on that pile of dirt that surrounds so many pools of water, staring into the depths of the pond. The horses finished drinking and seemed in no hurry to leave. They stamped their hooves and swished their tails to keep away the buzzing insects and grasshoppers.

From its nest across the pasture, hidden among the undergrowth by the tall trees, a Whip-poor-will kept up its plaintive call.

"What does that whip-poor-will say? Does anyone know? Have any of you ever seen one?" Lucas asked while glancing at the men.

Shifting their stance from one leg to the other, their eyes met, and each mumbled a few words and laughed nervously. A few offered an opinion.

"No. I've never seen one," said one.

"Don't know what they look like," said another.

"Wouldn't know what I was looking at if I came nose to nose with it," was the last reply.

Harlen answered. "I don't know what anyone else thinks, but to me it sounds like it's saying, "chip the widow's white oak." They stay hid in the daytime and come off their nest in late evening or just at daylight. But I've never seen one."

No other explanation was offered.

Several men lived and worked on the farm, slept in the bunkhouse, but took their meals in the main house. The actual numbers went up and down, depending on the season.

Skinner Bishop, his wife Hazel, and their son Wyatt lived on the Martin Place in a small house that had, at other times, been used by share-croppers. Skinner did odd jobs around the farm. He could build or fix anything, ride a horse, milk or brand a cow, and he helped Laura with chores she could not do.

On wash day, he would build a fire and place a rather large black iron kettle among the coals, shifting it around so its short legs would hold it straight. Then he would fill it with buckets of water. Clothes that had been washed in a tub of cold water and rubbed against the rubboard would be placed in the hot water as a final rinse before being hung on the clothesline and fastened with wooden clothes pens. Skinner always checked the wire clothesline to see if it was sagging. It seemed to always need tightening for wet clothes weighted it down.

Hazel helped Laura, when asked, and she had sent word with Skinner that she would appreciate Hazel's help in preparing food for the men for their trip north.

Aside from the main house with a peach and apple orchard, a large pear tree was just outside the fence gate. Close by was a mulberry tree whose limbs leaned away from the trunk of the tree and on which Harlen's youngest sister often sat fighting with the birds for each berry. There was a large garden also, and between both, they provided all the fruit and vegetables needed for the occupants.

Hogs and chickens were their source for meat, supplement-ed by wild turkeys that roamed freely and slept in trees, rabbits that ran and sought safety in their holes in the ground, squirrels whose huge nests were high in trees anchored to a limb, and fish that swam in the creek.

A few days later in the late afternoon, Joe and Harlen stood in the barnyard looking out across the open field where cattle and horses grazed. A low mountain, some few thousand feet high rose against the skyline. At its feet a meandering creek flowed past oak and cedar trees which grew on its bank and were fed by its water.

On a well-trod path, cattle made their way to the barn, fol-lowing each other lined up in a row, one behind the other, ready to be milked.

The collie dog named Shadow trotted behind them with a pleased expression on her face, knowing she had satisfactorily completed her job of rounding up the cattle and heading them toward the barn.

Still later that same afternoon, all the men who worked on the farm gathered in the barn lot. Some leaned against the fence while others sat on the top railing. Harlen had called the meeting to explain any doubts they might have, regarding details of the work load among the men who would remain on the farm during his absence.

Two men, one young and one older, sat up late that night discussing the best fields to cross to get the cattle to the sale barn. They planned on visiting the neighbors after breakfast.

Soft and welcoming early morning sunshine covered one side of the house, reaching down to the ground. It spread out across the barn lot, finally creeping under the roof of the lean-to where the wagon was sheltered.

Harlen had hitched the horses to the wagon and was seated holding the reins. Joe slowly and carefully eased his sore body onto the board which was the width of the wagon-bed and served as a seat.

With the click of his tongue the horses stepped forward. The farm wagon with its narrow iron wheels, which a few days ago was loaded with hay, was their conveyance. It passed slowly in front of the house with both men holding their gaze on the building.

Gone were the days when a surrey would stop by the white picket fence surrounding the house. Attached to the covering of the surrey was a border whose looped threads made a fringe on all four sides and swayed when soft winds passed by. A fringe edged blanket covered each horse from its forehead, down its back, stopping at the tail.

Gone also was the balcony from above the front entrance, as well as the pillars which held it up. A slanting roof had been erected to take its place and to cover the veranda. The roof was held up by tall, thin posts.

"Dad, why did they tear off the balcony? It just ruined the looks of the whole house."

"We couldn't get anyone to repair it." Joe looked at the empty place and sighed. "It needed a new roof. We couldn't get anybody to climb up there and replace the shingles. Roofers complained it was too steep. They were afraid to climb. Rainwater was leaking through and causing some damage."

"Well, while they were up there tearing it down they could have done some reroofing," Harlen said. "They were already half way to the top."

2

PAST VS PRESENT

Years had gone by, and Joe's inheritance was the land and all buildings that sat upon it. His siblings had taken their share from inside the house.

Very few dishes were left in the cupboard. Laura and one of her sisters-in-law played tug of war over a dish that little boy Harlen ate from. "Would you take the boy's dish?" Laura asked while holding on to it.

"Yes. I would," was the reply. Laura would not turn loose. Finally, the sister-in-law released her hold.

European wallpaper no longer adorned all rooms with its shiny surface. When the kitchen walls looked too dark from smoke from the cook stove, Laura put new covering on them.

She made a paste of flour and water and brushed a page of a newspaper with it then pressed the paper against the wall, smoothing out wrinkles and air pockets with a rag.

Harlen was a small boy when his grandparents died. He could barely remember what they looked like. He could vaguely remember his aunts and uncles coming to the house and carrying away furniture, beds, dishes, and even some clothing.

Joe and Laura refurnished the house and raised three more children. All girls. Their first three were boys.

Harlen was rather quiet and soft-spoken. He much preferred being outside, in the fields, riding Old Don or talking with the hired hands, some who were cousins, others not.

Joe was away a great deal on cattle buying trips and, Harlen and his mother were left to run the farm. They shared one special bond. Horses, mares, and colts came to them as if they were personal friends. They often trotted or ran to them whinnying and extending their heads to be rubbed.

Harlen and the hired hands worked in the fields planting or harvesting.

Laura walked among the cattle looking for those who needed to be milked. She sympathized with young calves rubbing their backs and talking to them when separating them from their mothers at weaning time. All this, while keeping an eye on her small children who followed her around the barn lot.

For several evenings she had stood looking across the gate and into the fields, waiting for her pregnant mare to come back to the barn. Each night she did not come. On the fourth day Laura opened the gate and started across the field looking for her. After about a mile the mare was found at the edge of the woods tangled up in vines. Laura pulled and tugged at the vines freeing her. The mare trotted back to the barn, barely in time for her foal to be born.

In the spring of nineteen twenty-seven, too much rain had fallen. Rivers and creeks were running full. Now in early autumn for several months past, not one drop of moisture had fallen from the sky. Deep cracks appeared in the ground. Laura and her children carried buckets of water to the garden to water the okra, tomatoes, lettuce, and cabbage. Onions and potatoes took up more garden space but received less water. Onion bulbs and potato eyes maturing underground retained some moisture.

Laura tended her garden with care, for her family depended on its crops, whether fresh or canned. She pulled weeds and hoed, and when she saw a rock, she picked it up and dropped it over the fence.

Memories of the garden and orchard at her childhood home came often. Vegetables and grapes ripened together. Clusters of dark blue grapes hanging from the vines grew along the fence which enclosed the garden, and, at times, she thought she could smell their sweet aroma.

In the orchard, apples were plucked from the limb or picked up off the ground. Dust was wiped off each one, then they were rubbed to a shine. They were placed in a bushel basket which her father picked up and set in his wagon, which had rubber tires. He drove to town and sold them to waiting customers.

The Depression of the late nineteen twentys still lingered into the nineteen thirties. Money was tight and seemed to be disappearing since once it was spent there was no replacement.

Occasionally, Joe wanted a field made available for cotton. It was a cash crop when he was running short of money. One year in its abundance, it overflowed the out buildings. The last of the picking was stored against one side of the hallway of the house and reached halfway to the ceiling.

A few days later it was loaded into the wagon which was pulled by mules and taken to the cotton gin in the town of Wild Cherry. There the machine would pull the soft cotton from the boles then pull away the fibrous, creamy white substance covering its seeds. It then would be bailed and sold.

Joe and Laura discussed money. She disagreed with him in his notion to borrow two-thousand-dollars from the bank in Calico Rock pledging the farm as security. He borrowed the money anyway. The loan was known only to the two of them, and it weighed heavily on their minds.

At times when she sat at her Singer sewing machine with her foot pressing the treadle, words came to mind that Joe's father had said to her. "Don't let Joe borrow money. If he does, he'll lose the farm." Concentrating on the up and down motion of the needle, she sewed patches on the knees of Joe's denim overalls and on the elbows of Harlen's cotton shirts.

On the front page of the newspaper, Germany and her aggressions were measured by columns. Announcers over the radio disturbed the airwaves with talk of war.

She was the first daughter born into a household with five boys. Two older and three younger. In time she would have four sisters and two more brothers.

They learned to play musical instruments. She played the organ and accordion. Her father John Lee Foster played the fiddle, as did her oldest brother Rob who also played a harmonica. All joined in the singing, and Laura blended her voice with the others. They gathered around the organ which sat close to a window. When it was open, her young siblings would climb through it upon abandoning the swing on the ell shaped veranda when they heard singing. Their small voices joined the others, and the sound drifted through and around the large house and across its yard. She grew up with music and singing and laughter.

Her older brothers had married, and when Laura became serious about matrimony, she talked with her father and told him she wanted to marry the other man, the school teacher. Her father said she should marry "that other man" whose family had land, that young man of German descent with blue eyes and hair the color of sand with a reddish tint whose nickname was Sorrel Top.

Joe was her second choice for a husband, but she obeyed her father. They were married at her home and Joe took his new bride to the Haughn farm in a carriage with her horse tied behind. Her side-saddle, trunk, and dresser, which was a wedding present from her father, would be brought to the farm at the first opportunity. She settled into the household, mixing song and laughter of the Irish into the stoic German family.

She looked after her father-in-law, treating him special. Once when he was invited to dinner at one of his daughter's houses and arrived back home without having eaten, she was concerned. When asked why he did not eat, he replied, he didn't like what she had cooked. "She knows I don't like that stuff," he said while shaking his head and making a sour face.

She walked toward her cookstove. "What would you like to eat, Mr. Haughn? I'll cook it for you."

The Haughn farm proper contained two-hundred and fifty acres with a deed signed by President James Buchanan. But with government leased acreage on the bayou, it was just under one thousand acres with creeks and their branches coursing over the land. A meadow, trees, and low mountains framed the open view from the kitchen window. On the property were a few houses which were rented to farmers who had no land of their own.

They lived on and worked certain acres, while sharing the bounty with the owner.

When Joe's father William Miller Haughn married Margaret Jane Wyatt, daughter of John J. Wyatt and Christiana Duckworth, he was named a partner in his father-in-law's business. A new sign went up on the front of the building. It now read "Wyatt and Haughn Mercantile." Their inventory included McGuffey Readers, among many other items which people of that time period found useful in their lives. Money was loaned at ten percent interest.

The store was a short distance from the house that was built for Joe's father, which Joe inherited at his father's death. The deed, drawn up years before, stipulated that Joe, 'for love and affection' would inherit the property, providing that his father William Miller Haughn and his mother Margaret Jane Wyatt Haughn could stay in the house and be cared for until their deaths. Upon failure to carry out the stipulation, the deed would become null and void.

From the kitchen Laura would walk across the screened-in porch, down the hall, and into a bedroom where she would look after Margaret Jane, who in later years became ill and required much care. Once she asked one of her sisters-in-law to help look after her own mother. The sister-in-law said, "No. I hate old people."

Caught kissing Joe in the hallway before his father and he left on a cattle buying trip, she was embarrassed by her in-laws. They laughed and advised her, "Don't carry on so. He'll be back."

Harlen often climbed over a fence and walked along a sunken, abandoned road while hunting rabbits, pheasants, or absent bovine. He was aware the ancient road led off toward the now sparsely populated town of Wild Cherry. It was of little concern to him, for in his lifetime it had always been there and no one ever talked about it. On this day, Old Don, Shadow, and he were on the trail of a pregnant cow who would be calving any moment.

The long-ago road, worn down three feet deep by travelers crossing the open land, led past the mercantile store and toward the town of Wild Cherry, which once was of modest size with many stores and three hotels.

Animals, long before the buffalo and Indians, long before the pioneers, soldiers, horses and wagons, traveled through leaving foot prints while carving a pathway to be followed.

Ancestors carried money from the old country to purchase land in the new country. They built it up through agriculture and commerce. In time the land and wealth were passed on to a new generation. They made new roads and built up more wealth. Through them, towns, cities, law, churches, and schools came into existence.

Through wars, depressions, and financial swings, both money and land were lost. Some would recoup, though it might take a while. Others would never get back what they lost. Hope, determination, and strength of body and mind had to be found to go forward with what remained.

Harlen was born in the ashes of what was left of a once well-off family. He had the work ethic of his father, could be stubborn when he thought he was right, and preferred listening to talking. His mother had a quick smile, was kind, cheerful and soft spoken. He inherited those qualities from her.

He had some knowledge of what the past must have been like. The house he was born in was built for and belonged to his grandparents. It was furnished by them, and upon their deaths, became part of their estate and was divided up and disbursed among their children.

All that remained were a few dishes and a chest about four feet high that no one wanted. Among the furniture Joe and Laura purchased to replace what was divided through the estate was a huge rosewood wardrobe, a roll-top desk, and two heavy parlor chairs which were placed in front of the fireplace. As a young boy, Harlen was sure two people could easily sit in each one.

Harlen stared at the daguerreotype picture of Margaret Duckworth Wyatt that hung from a nail on the wall. The pretty, oval faced woman is wearing spade shaped, dangly earrings with three diamonds down the middle. Under her chin, pinned to her high neck dress, is a small broach with a large diamond in the middle surrounded by nine smaller stones. A gold chain with a cross attached at the end hangs past her bosom.

Laura came into the room, and he called to her to also look at the picture. "Mother, who has all that jewelry that Grandma is wearing?"

"The necklace was part of the estate," she replied while studying the picture. "I never saw any of the jewelry except the gold chain. I don't know what happened to the rest of it. Margaret was quiet young when that picture was taken."

Once, when Harlen was visiting a cousin, mention was made of a trunk that had belonged to John J. Wyatt. Expressing a desire to see it, he was led into a room where it sat against the wall, covered with a scarf. The cousin removed the cloth and quickly lifted the lid. He stared in awe and guessed the trunk was maybe three feet in length and about a foot in height. So quickly did she slam the lid back down that the eyes and brain could only focus on its near emptiness. And as quickly, the scarf was laid back over it.

But Harlen seldom thought about the past. The mercantile store was gone. The house had been altered, the surrey was gone as were the fringe blankets, and, he suspected, most of the money. He was young, handsome, strong and inquisitive. He knew he walked in their footsteps, arose each morning as they did, looked out the same window, walked down the same steps, and when the day was over, lay down to sleep in the room they had slept in, but his ancestors belonged to the past. He did not have the privilege of knowing many of them. They now lay sleeping in their graves waiting to be awakened by the blast from Gabriel's trumpet.

In the period in time in which Harlen lived, it was a new day with different work requirements. His dad and he were on their way to talk to the neighbors regarding a pressing need in his family.

3

OVER PRIVATE PROPERTY

The wagon traveled up the road following a fence line until they reached a gravel highway. Harlen shook the reins and the horses quickened their gait to a trot. The iron wheels rolling over gravel made a noise that could be heard a quarter of a mile away. Dust rose up behind them, and birds darted from the road.

Joe filled the time with talk for there was much he wished to say. "At the stockyard you'll meet a buyer named Waymon Jenkins. He's a hard-nosed peckerwood when it comes to money. You'll be asking ten cents a pound for cows and twelve cents for yearlings and bulls. He'll laugh and tell you nobody gets that kind of money. Stand your ground. Don't let him talk you into taking anything less."

Harlen's mouth opened as if to say something, but he was interrupted.

"Let me tell you something son," his dad added in a softer voice, while rubbing the injury to his back and taking a couple of deep breaths. "I've heard the government is buying up cattle, digging a trench, driving them in it, then shootin'em. I want our cattle sold while we still can. With the shape the country's in and now here in Arkansas with highway construction being run by the federal government, this state most likely will go bankrupt 'cause it can't afford to pay for the state bonds. It's a tough time Son. Here it is nineteen thirty-six and no one has any money. Everyone has land and cattle, and nobody wants any more of either one."

Then they rode in silence for a while on this pleasant morning. Harlen was thinking about his dad. How he had thought of everything, step-by-step all the way to the sale barn. He was aware of the vast difference in age and experience to call on.

In his fifty years Joe had seen, been part of, been right more times than wrong, and experienced knocks and disappointment that all people bump into. He learned from his dad. They were a team in the cattle buying business.

But for an eighteen-year old, Harlen possessed wisdom from many sources. Shrewd in how many acres should be devoted to hay, how many were needed for corn, and which fields should lay fallow.

He learned how to aggravate his sister and leave the house and head to the barn before she started whining and tattling. Once after they had had a spat, he left the house quickly, and, while heading to the barn, called out, "Whiner, Whiner, Whiner!" The sound carried through the open windows and wafted past the ears of those inside. Hearing a door slam, he ran the rest of the way and jumped on the back of Old Don. They headed out across the pasture.

He set a price of five dollars to break horses for the saddle for anyone who asked, as long as they were willing to pay him the five dollars. This took courage and planning. Leading them to the barn and into a stable, he then would climb up in the loft where he removed a plank from over the stable. Holding on to a rafter, he slowly let himself down until he was sitting on the back of the animal. It was up to the horse to decide how soon he would accept the blanket, the saddle and, the rider.

But for many nights, he had stared at the ceiling unable to sleep, thinking about the men, the wagon loaded with supplies, the animals, the distance, and how he could accomplish all this in four days.

A well-kept road led off the highway and Joe broke the silence. "Pull off here. This is our first stop."

By mid-afternoon they were on their way to the fourth farm they would cross over. All had gone well.

Harlen stood by the side of his dad while he talked to the neighbors. He was three inches short of his dad's six-foot height. His muscles were taut from pitching loose hay, hooking baled hay, carrying new-born calves, and breaking bucking horses. He weighed one hundred and thirty-two pounds.

All cows, horses, and cowboys would travel over four different farms of fenced private property. The land was mostly flat except for a few hillocks, but there were two creeks to cross – one narrow, one wide. In late autumn there would still be plenty of grass, though some might be turning brown.

Joe assured the neighbors they would take down the fence to let the cattle through then put it back up. Each farmer gave his guarantee their cattle would be moved to another field, and their dogs would be pinned up while the cattle passed through.

"There'll be no damages except hoof prints in the soil," Joe assured each one. No money was mentioned by either party. It was neighbor helping neighbor.

Joe bragged that Harlen would be in charge of the drive. "He's eighteen now," he said.

Harlen smiled at the 'well wishes' and was surprised that his dad would offer praise, for he almost never did. Still, Harlen wished he hadn't said anything for he was a little embarrassed.

Joe stood at his roll-top desk trying to remember which drawer he had placed the papers in. Opening and closing three without finding them, he moved back a few steps and ran his fingers through his hair. After a moment he bent forward to open a bottom drawer, which sent a sharp pain down his back. He grunted. There the papers were, and gathering them up, he slowly stood. He filled his pen with ink by inserting it in the inkwell and drawing the black fluid slowly up to the top. With paper and pen in hand, the door to his office swung shut. He went looking for Harlen.

Joe stood at the open door speaking a few words to his son who was in his bedroom and had removed his shirt in preparation for bed. "I'm sure you've picked your drivers. Ones you can trust."

Without waiting for a reply, he entered the room.

From the papers in his hand, he handed Harlen a Bill of Sale for the cattle. "Give this to Waymon," he instructed.

For the second paper he said, "This is the contract that Waymon and I signed. We both initialed it, but I need to scratch out my name and put yours on it since you're the one who will deliver the cattle to him." He pressed the paper to the wall and drew a thin line across his name and wrote in Harlen's name.

"Now we both need to initial it." Joe handed him the pen. "Give the buyer, that old peckerwood, my regards." Joe chuckled and started down the hall.

Resting his head on a feather pillow and turning over in his mind how to do all that was being asked of him, caused doubt to creep into Harlen's thoughts. There in the darkness, for a while, he wrestled with uncertainty and fear as he thought of all the things that could go wrong. He had slept very little when day-light crept up behind the mountains.

Laying a change of clothes on a newspaper then taking down his chaps from a nail driven into the wall, he buckled them around his waist then fitted them on his legs. He then put on a leather vest and placed the papers in an inside pocket along with his wallet. Reaching for the rolled-up newspaper and leaving his bedroom, he walked through the screened-in porch to the kitchen.

Laura, small in stature with hazel eyes and black hair which was pulled back, rolled in a bun, then fastened by large hair pins, hurried between the stove and table. Her apron covered most of her dress which was only a few inches above the ankle. She set dishes and pans of food in front of those gathered there.

Harlen sliced open two biscuits and laid them on his plate close to the fried eggs and a thick slice of ham. He then poured red-eye gravy over all. No words were exchanged while they ate, but when he finished, pushed his plate away, and scooted his chair back in, his mother called his name.

"Harlen," she said softly, "Be careful. Don't get hurt."

"I'll be careful, Mother. Don't you worry."

Through the open door, she watched her son walk toward the fence. On his left side she noticed a slight limp. When he was born that foot was turned up almost touching his leg. The doctor told her the baby would never walk. Every night with downward strokes, she rubbed his foot until he began to cry. Eighteen years later the limp was hardly noticeable. That leg kicked forward ever so slightly, and his walk looked a little like a cocky swagger.

Spurs had been fitted over their boots. Three of the riders and he crossed the yard heading toward the picket fence from which time and weather had stripped away all the paint. Old Don and several other horses and riders waited on the other side. All wore spurs except Claude.

Joe waited by the gate, giving the last instructions to his son whom he was trusting with a big man-sized job. "Push the cattle hard on the first day. Get them off familiar land. On day four, Waymon will be waiting at the sale barn for you and the cattle. You'll be paid by check. Take it to the bank in West Plains. It will be on a Saturday and they should be open. Cash it and pay John Baxter for his fifteen head. Keep the money on you at all times. Get a good meal and a good night's sleep then hurry home."

Harlen, Price, Lucas, and the other riders untied the horses and swung a leg over their backs. He felt a great weight settling on his shoulders. From the saddle he waved to his dad, and seeing his mother on the veranda, waved to her. Then he turned to the others and said, "Men, we're no longer farmhands. Now we're trail-driving, cattle-pushing cowboys."

4

TRAIL DRIVING, CATTLE PUSHING COWBOY'S

The six men walked their mounts in silence. Each one wondered at the task ahead for none had ever trailed that many cattle that far. Of all the men, Price knew more about the drive than any of the rest for he had read books and seen Saturday afternoon picture shows about old-time cattle drives. He had a general idea of how to go about getting the cattle to the sale barn some forty miles up the road, and he could help Harlen, in case he was asked. The age group varied from early seventies down to sixteen. Each appeared to be excited at this new adventure, if somewhat apprehensive.

Bellowing and mooing suddenly could be heard from behind them. Mr. Baxter and his two sons came up the road with their fifteen head, eager to join the others.

When they were even with the men, Old Don stepped out in a fast walk, and Harlen gave instructions to the men. "Bring'em forward," he said then rode on ahead.

Presently he saw his cattle bunched along the fence and held there by other men who would remain behind. "Take down the fence. Let the cattle out," he yelled.

They had to be driven out onto the road for they could hear the other cows mooing as they came closer, and all heads were turned in that direction. But they joined together and walked at a steady pace.

Skinner, pipe stem clamped between his teeth and smoke curling upwards, and his son Wyatt followed in the loaded wagon pulled by two sturdy mules. He had started packing the wagon a few days earlier with items he thought might be needed for the trip. Harlen placed the newspaper, with his clean change of clothes, under the seat.

Laura and Hazel had taken down from the rafter in the smoke house two large smoked hams and wrapped them in clean cloths then in newspapers. They did the same for thick salt bacon. Buckets with handles and lids were filled with cooked beans. A large sack filled with potatoes and onions was stowed in the bed of the wagon. Biscuits and cornbread were packed in boxes. The women had baked cakes and made skillets full of fried apple pies. Cinnamon and chocolate rolls completed the sweeter side. Skinner placed the food in the wagon.

Laura cut a clean flour sack into strips for bandages, should they be needed. The available medicine was rubbing alcohol, iodine, and tape. All were packed in a small box and placed beside the growing items that had been stowed under the wagon seat.

Seventy-one head of cattle presented several problems before they reached open land. The gravel road was not wide enough to accommodate many. Several ran toward the trees and had to be rounded up. Some just stopped in the middle of the road and were loudly encouraged to keep moving, with language often heard in a barn yard by aggravated cowboys. When the cows played deaf, more forceful means were applied. At times, cowboys, cows, and calves, headed in all directions.

Tanner Sullivan drove up in a shiny black 1929 pickup. The vehicle stopped, and Harlen guided Old Don to its side. The two men exchanged a few words for they were longtime friends.

"I'd like to follow along," Tanner said. "I'll stay on the road, but I'll keep an eye on your location." He glanced at the livestock then at the men in the saddle. "I won't be far behind if you need me. This looks like fun."

"Okay. Then follow along," Harlen said with a chuckle. "Glad you think it's going to be fun. I sure hope you're right. We're pretty soon going to get away from this road and cut across the fields. We'll continue east until we get to Viola, then we'll turn north. From time to time I can get a view of the main road, and I'll look for you." Harlen was pleased to have the vehicle along in case of an injury to one of the men. It could also carry young calves if they fell behind during the journey.

Pulling back on Old Don's reins caused the animal to rear up, balancing his weight on his hind legs, then paw the air with the front legs. Settling down with four hooves on the ground, a gentle touch with the toe of Harlen's boot made him lunge forward in a gallop.

They traveled at a slow but steady pace, even while rounding up young bulls who had decided to bolt for the trees. The new cowboys were busy looking for a vantage spot close to the herd, trying to convince them to go forward.

The early morning sun spread its rays over everyone and everything. It was obviously going to be a long, hot day.

Harlen, hat pushed back and hand resting on the butt of his rifle, trained his eyes on a hill and to the right of a large walnut tree. He had seen something move. His spurs touched the sides of Old Don, and the horse trotted up to Price Turley, the point man for the first day's drive.

"Do you see something moving around on that hill to the east"? he asked him.

"Sure do. Looks like a pack of dogs." While their eyes were trained on the horizon, other canines appeared.

"The one in front looks like a big, male wolf to me." A trace of alarm sounded in Harlen's voice. The new arrivals joined with those already there. "I was just about to fall asleep last night, and with my window open I heard howling. I thought it was coyotes." The two men stared at the hillside trying to count the moving dogs.

"How many?" Price asked.

"I counted eight. It's a pack of wolves I'm sure. They'll be after the calves," Harlen said. He turned in the saddle to look back at the herd which included old cows, young cows, calves, heifers, and young bulls. "Ride back to the others and alert them to the situation. Tell them to bunch the cows and calves together. Tell them to push the cattle. We need to make as many miles today as we can."

Price galloped off on his half-tamed palomino. He was born on Harlen's birthday exactly nineteen years earlier and had always wanted to be a cowboy. He was now weathered and tanned by the outdoors and strong as a bull.

Harlen stayed in the front, keeping his eyes on the distant movements. While watching, he noticed the advance of the lead wolf, head held high, eyes fixed on the herd. Although some distance away, their keen hearing and sense of smell had picked up the scent of cattle and man, and their ears twitched at the sound of many hooves pounding the earth. Harlen soon counted five more of various sizes.

Old Don, the faithful quarter horse, snorted when a gust of wind blew the wild, pungent odor of the wolves under his nose.

Price, having delivered the message, spurred his horse to a gallop. Lucas, astride his smooth riding grey stallion, hurried to catch up to him. Together they reached Harlen's side, slowed their horses to a walk, and turned their heads to watch the wolves.

The lead wolf stopped and lay down on his stomach. The others, smaller and younger, became playful, cavorting and running a short way from the others then running back. Taking his eyes off the herd just long enough to regain control over the young ones, he nipped and cuffed a young pup, sending him rolling and yelping.

The cowboys drove the herd on but kept a steady eye on their surroundings. While they watched, a female wolf trotted into the pack. The male got up and acknowledged her presence. Then all of them lifted their heads and let out a frightening howl. Playtime was over. When the howling stopped, the large grey wolf trotted in the opposite direction of the herd with the others following.

"Are they leaving?" Lucas asked hopefully.

"They're just changing locations," Price said.

"They'll be back when they get hungry." Harlen shook his head anticipating a near catastrophe.

The wolves disappeared into the woods. Everyone - cowboys, horses, cows – all of them, from time to time cast a wary eye toward the tree line for none wanted to see them following the herd.

Cowboys spurred their horses and chased after the animals who cared little which way they were headed. But occasionally, when Harlen looked at the whole picture, all seemed to be moving in the same direction, though slower than he would have liked.

He circled the entire herd conversing with the men as he met them. Riding ahead of the lead animals and sometimes a mile or so beyond, he studied the land, noticing low places, large rocks, downed timber or anything that cattle or wagon might need to avoid.

Riding side by side with Price he said, "We need to push on for another hour or two. Turn the cattle toward the hills and take them to the bayou. There's clear running water there, even at this time of year. I'll ride on ahead and find a place to camp."

Trailing cattle by the hour through dust and over grass where they often stopped to graze, plus watching the timberline for the wolves, kept the men in the saddle though some were anxious to dismount. All were tired and hungry.

In another half mile they would be leaving Haughn property. They could see the fence which was the dividing line. It was just beyond a wide creek with two feet of clear flowing water and a sandy bed.

Harlen squatted down on the bank and pushed his canteen under the water, watching it fill up while bubbles floated to the surface. A few feet away Old Don waded in on all fours. Lowering his head into a little eddy where water trickled more slowly, he slurped loudly. "We'll stop here for the night," Harlen shouted when the men were within hearing distance.

All the animals wanted water, and they headed for the creek, waded into it, and drank. Seventy-one head of cattle plus horses, including the two mules who waded in wagon and all, pretty well filled up the creek.

Harlen observed Skinner and Wyatt in the creek in the wagon, sitting ramrod straight upon the seat. "That sure makes a pretty picture," he said with a laugh. "Bet that's the first time you've sat in water without getting wet."

Skinner laughed with him. "Wyatt and I'll get our fill when my mules get their fill," he said.

Utah, long legged and skinny, was the official camp cook. He had built a fire but was waiting for the water in the creek to settle down. He kept an eye on the mud and sand as it drifted back to the bottom. Dipping his tin cup into the water he sipped it, testing the contents for sand. Several times he poured it out. When he was satisfied that it was clear and drinkable, he picked up three buckets and walked upstream from where the animals had stood. Bending over he filled the buckets then walked back to the campfire.

He noticed Price heading to the creek carrying the coffeepot and another bucket. He shot him a hard look. Price did not look at Utah so he didn't see the sour expression on his face, though his disposition was always a little sour. He would have preferred to have the cooking detail to himself.

Price had not asked if he could help with the cooking. He had just picked up a spoon, lifted the lid to the bean pot, and started stirring. Next, he poured yellow cornmeal into a pan, cracked an egg and dropped in the contents, poured in a little water, then dipped into the lard bucket for a generous helping of fat. He stirred it all together, poured it into a pan, then set the pan in the coals.

Utah gave him another hard look but said nothing. He actually liked Price. It's just that the kitchen was his job. The other thing was that he was irritable to begin with, preferring his own company and the quiet that goes with being alone. Utah came from a large family and his mother needed him in the kitchen. She taught him how and what to cook and he found he liked kitchen work. He could cook just about anything, and his cakes were lighter and tenderer than his mother's. She always called upon him to do the baking.

With two of them preparing the meal, the smell of coffee awoke the appetite. After the horses were watered, unsaddled, and staked, and the cattle had stopped wandering, each cowboy picked up a plate and all hurried to the camp fire. With ham frying in hot grease, cornbread baking in a pan in the coals alongside potatoes, anticipation brought forth smiles and soft laughter from young and old. Price looked at those around him who were holding plates. "Dig in," he said.

Harlen held up his hand. "First, we need to give thanks to my mom and Mrs. Bishop who cooked for two days so we would have food to eat while on this trip," he said.

With one voice the men hollered, "Thanks, Mom. Thanks, Mrs. Bishop."

"And God!" a strong voice stated with conviction. It came from an older, stooped and white-haired cowpuncher who knew where the source of all food came from. He was called Gramps.

Neither Harlen nor his father knew his real name. He was working on the Haughn farm when Harlen was born. Everyone liked the old gentleman and treated him as if he were their own kin.

"Let's bow our heads in reverence to our Maker," Gramps said, lowering his head. "God, thank you for the food, for man and beasts. Amen." All echoed his Amen.

"We'll sleep in the open tonight away from the trees," Harlen said while drinking deeply from his tin cup. "Bring the horses in closer and stake them."

He got up and walked to the edge of the men and their shadows and whistled a call that was familiar to Old Don who trotted up to him and stopped. Harlen withdrew a handful of corn from his pocket and put it under the nose of the faithful animal. He swung his head up and down a couple of times then ate from his hand.

There was little grumbling while they ate. All asked for second and third cups of coffee. The campfire burned brightly for a while, and some of the men struck up a conversation.

"This here herd of cattle we're driving to the feed lot is mighty fine stock," Gramps said. "Joe is a cattle buyer and one of the best. He went with his dad on buying trips when he was a young kid with sandy colored hair, before it turned black. He learned how to choose each animal, what to watch for when looking them over, which ones to keep, and which ones to avoid. To him, cattle is money on four legs. He buys the animals, drives 'em home, fattens 'em up, and sells 'em."

Price knew cattle and nodded his head in agreement with Gramps. "This farm buys, sells, and keeps the finest lookin' cattle I've ever seen," he said.

Unlike his dad who saw them as a group, Harlen saw each one and had even named a few: Old Bossy. Big Eyes. Swish Tail. He seldom joined in idle conversation for he was comfortable in his own thoughts. But he was eager to hear other words spoken by other men, turning them over in his mind, accepting or rejecting their merit. He had a ready laugh when someone said or did something funny, and he could laugh at himself when appropriate.

The evening had begun to cool down and cicadas were tuning up from their perch in the trees. They were loud even at a distance.

Tex was the first one to set down his plate. "I don't know about anybody else, but I'm turnin' in," he said. He got up, and the rest of the men followed. Each man picked a spot to lie down on. Bedrolls and blankets were spread on the ground. All were aware that somewhere behind the trees was a pack of wolves that could only mean trouble.

Harlen pulled off his boots, scooted down, and stretched out in his bedroll. His saddle served as a pillow, and he lay listening to the slow steps of the cattle as they circled, before stopping altogether. Cows, young heifers, bulls, and three skinny doges bellowed softly, and one by one, they lay down. For a while, soft bellowing and snores from men, lying on the ground wrapped in blankets, and night insects were all that could be heard.

He lay looking up at the millions of stars that lit the empty space between Heaven and Earth. His head jerked up to watch a blazing meteor making its way across the sky, leaving a red streak behind. When his head rested once again on his saddle, he thought about the day that had just ended and tomorrow. "One day gone," he whispered to himself. In his mind's eye, he could see his dad's blue eyes looking straight at him. He wondered if he could carry out his wishes. "I've got to," he whispered. "I've just got to."

Turning on his side, he put an arm under his head. Unable to sleep, he listened to the many different snores and the wind as it drifted through branches on the trees. High pitched howls broke the silence. Each man came awake, reached for his firearm, and chambered a bullet. Horses stomped around as far as their tether would let them, and the cattle began to stir.

Harlen raised up, pulled on his boots, then stood up. "We better post guards around the cattle," he said. "Three men should do – each taking a three-hour shift. I'll take the first shift." Several volunteered. Price said he would build up the fire and put on some coffee.

All too often several different howls could be heard. At times it seemed they were closer to the animals then at other times. Yet when all the canines lifted their heads to join together, it was hard to tell which direction they came from. Danger was sensed by man and animal.

5

EYES FOLLOWING
THE HERD

Sleep was little to none. The men crawled out of their bedrolls
sleepy-eyed, stumbling around, some grumbling about not
getting any sleep, while others expressed concern about what the
wolves would do and when.

The sky of early morning looked pale with a cool wind blowing through the camp. The two cooks already had bacon siz-
zling and biscuits browning when men shook out their bedrolls,
rolled them up and tied them behind their saddles. They went in
groups to the creek to wash before handing a plate to Utah and
a cup to Price.

Utah wore a more pleasant expression on his face as he placed
the food on each place. He had begun to learn how to work with
Price in their outdoor kitchen, and at times a smile could be seen
on his face, if one looked quick enough.

"Men we need to cover some ground today," Harlen said while waiting his turn in line. "We didn't get very far yesterday and we have to be at the sale barn Saturday."

Standing by the fire Harlen turned his back to the rest of the men, dabbed a biscuit in red-eye gravy, and bit into it. In a low voice, he spoke to Price who tipped the coffee pot and filled each cup to the brim.

"I want you to go on ahead and take down the fence," he said. "When all the cattle are through, put it back up. I've been watching Lucas. Take him with you. He's young, inexperienced and a good kid. He's also a good horseman, but he doesn't know squat about anything other than his stallion. I'll give him credit for that. He sure knows how to handle the gray. Teach him there's more to cowboying than sittin' on a horse." He paused to take another bite of the biscuit and stared into his plate. Then cutting up the egg he scooted it into the gravy. After another bite he continued. "Tell him he has to learn how to take care of animals, read their minds, and how to stay one step ahead of 'em." Not all animals are docile. Some are stubborn. Some are hard to handle and some are just plain mean. He has to learn how to take care of all kinds. You know that but he don't." He soaked up the last of the gravy with his biscuit and put it in his mouth. "One last thing," he said as Price filled his own cup and poured the last few drops of the hot black coffee into Harlen's. "Tell him he needs to get used to the smell of barnyards, stables, and stalls. Tell him to keep a pitchfork and shovel handy to muck out the barn."

Then he turned around, and to the rest of the men he said, "Eat while you can, then get on your horses and get the cattle headed across the creek. Price, you and Lucas hurry on ahead and open up the fence. Skinner, Wyatt and you head out as soon as you're loaded." Harlen knew what chores needed to be done. They were arranged clearly in his mind, and there was no hesitation in voicing them.

Price picked up the fencing pliers from the wagon. Lucas and he left in a gallop.

A young steer from the middle of the herd had worked his way forward and was in front leading the restless, trotting animals across the creek. Price and Lucas galloped on ahead to unlatch the barbed wire gate and pull it to one side. As soon as it was wide open, the cows and calves stepped through, pouring into the neighbor's field.

When the last cow and horse had gone through the opening, they pulled the fence back to the main post and looped wire around it, being careful to avoid the barbs. When they were satisfied the gate was securely closed, they galloped on ahead.

"Lucas," Price said, "When we get to West Plains, you need to buy yourself a pair of leather gloves. See, like mine." He held up both hands fitted with tan colored cow skin gloves. "Barbed wire fences are the devil to work with."

"Yes. I found that out," he answered. "I've got a few stab wounds. Maybe when we get to town, I can find a store that sells gloves."

"I'm sure you can and I'll go with you."

Lucas smiled.

Price spent his money on his horse and himself. He owned several pairs of leather gloves; at least one pair had boots the same color. His saddle had touches of silver here and there, and his horse ate grain from a leather bag instead of off the ground like most of the animals did. He had never mentioned a woman's name - except his mother's - from whom he occasionally received a letter.

The cooking utensils had been tossed in the wagon and the dish water emptied on the coals. Skinner lifted the lash into the air, and with a quick jerk of his arm, a sound of a loud pop raced past the ears. The mules started out in a run. Pans that had not been properly secured, rattled loudly.

Muddy water flowed down the creek bed after cattle, horses, and wagon had crossed it. But muddy or clear, it drifted over gravel and around boulders. Half a mile downstream, it followed its course calmly and flowed so clear, one would never know it had been disturbed.

Cattle, horses, wagon, and men were moving forward in the early morning. Dust followed the herd, stirred up from the many hooves that tromped the earth. The cattle were not bunched, for the fields they traveled over provided more open space. The wolves were silent. Birds sang. Cattle mooed. Saddles squeaked. Tex sang about "An Old Cowhand," and was accompanied by others who knew the words.

Price and Lucas caught up to the men. "Hey," Price called out. "Is that Gene Autry or Roy Rogers singin'? I didn't know they had joined up. Where are they? I'd like to meet 'em."

"It's just me singing," Tex drawled. His dark, curly hair reached down to his collar, and a big smile spread across his handsome face. "Some others were helpin' me."

"Well, go on. Don't let me stop you. It sounded pretty good."

When they reached Viola and turned the cattle north, wolf howls had still not been heard. Traveling without stopping, by early afternoon they reached the Missouri border.

Cowboys were tired, hot, dusty, and hungry, but Harlen pushed on for a few more hours. Another fence was cut, pulled back, and laid on the ground. The two cowboys stood patiently while cattle, wagon, and men passed through.

Harlen kept his eyes on the herd and also looked for a place to camp for the night. He scanned all directions looking for the canines, but they kept out of sight. Borders meant nothing to the hungry wolves. He knew they had followed the herd into Missouri. He also knew they were out there in the wooded areas, for Old Don sometimes acted skittish, taking unnecessary steps, stepping sideways, and letting out occasional snorts.

When the sun began its downward spiral in the west, they were within sight of the fence that would be taken down so the cattle could cross over another field before they reached the sale barn.

On this, the second night, they took advantage of a creek which provided water for man and beast. Although narrow with a rather steep bank, it appeared to be waist deep on a man. They would camp there for the night, again away from the tree line.

The wagon, with its narrow iron wheels, could be heard some distance away. Utah and Price awaited its arrival, and when it did arrive, Price yelled to Utah - "Break out the food!" not to Claude who couldn't boil an egg and was just walking past.

Claude pretended not to hear. He unhitched the mules and led them to water. Picking up a rather large rock, he pounded the soft dirt of the creek bank, breaking it down for better access to the flowing stream.

Price climbed upon the wagon, opened the lid of the wooden box containing the meat, and lifted out a large chunk of ham. The wooden box was heavily padded with sheets of metal on the inside, from the bottom of the lid to all sides, including the very bottom. It held cold temperatures very well, even in hot weather.

He built a fire on the open ground, set an iron grate over it, then propped up each end with leftover sticks that he had gathered.

Opening the sack of potatoes, Price poured some on the ground. When a tall, lanky cowboy walked by, he volunteered him to help Utah with the peeling. When Claude returned from the creek and had staked the mules, Price handed him the empty coffee pot, pointed to the creek, and said, "Fill it."

When he returned with the pot, Price handed him a pan and said, "Help set the table. Take this to the wagon and put it down." Pots and pans filled with food were placed on the bed of the wagon next to the blue metal plates, forks, and knives. The large coffee pot was the last item brought to the table.

"Come and get it!" Claude called out. He helped himself to pinto beans, cornbread, fried potatoes, and a thick slice of ham. Sitting down on the ground, he crossed his legs and proceeded to cut the meat into cowboy-size portions.

Price was the last one to fill his plate, for he had taken a large container to the creek and filled it with water which he set over the flames of his fire. When it came to food, he liked everything clean, and even as a young man, he would keep an eye on the cooks. Eventually, while watching, he learned how to prepare food, then wash in hot water anything the food had touched.

Harlen had known Price for a long time, and while relying on his own knowledge and skills, on one or two occasions he had asked Price for his opinion. He was totally confident he would receive an honest answer. He also was in awe of his cooking skills.

Utah was the only other man he knew who liked to be in the kitchen - except to eat.

He remembered hearing his dad talk about camp fires when on a trip to buy cattle. He had laughed and said, "In the early days, the only cooking known to man was a rabbit roasting on a spit."

Wolf howls had not been heard since morning. Some began to wonder if - and hoped that - they had lost interest in the cattle and gone away. The men seemed more relaxed while sitting around the campfire drinking coffee.

As they did on the first night, John Baxter and his two adult sons sat on the ground a short distance from the others, eating food they had brought with them. They poured coffee from their own coffee pot. The boys lay on their stomachs listening to talk among the group next to the wagon.

"Do you think there'll be another cattle drive?" Lucas asked excitedly. "I like all this. I'd like to go on another one." He waved a hand at the men and the wagon.

"That's hard to say," Gramps said waving his cup around. "With the trouble our country's in right now, it might be a while." Setting down his cup, he stared into space for a few moments while fingering the rolled brim of his hat. After a thoughtful moment, he placed it back on his head.

"We don't have a lot of cattle left," Harlen said.

6

CAMPFIRE STORIES

"Joe is the buyer," Gramps spoke up while rising slowly to a standing position. "He learned from his dad. They would leave on horseback with their bedrolls tied behind the saddle. Sometimes they were gone for days. Joe must have been in his early twenties. He was a tall, slim young man with sandy colored hair and pale blue eyes. He was in his late thirties when his hair began to turn black. It started at the scalp, working its way down to the end. It looked funny so he usually wore his Stetson."

Gramps sat back down. "I remember his dad. Mr. Haughn," then he stopped and looked at Price. "You got any more coffee?" he asked. When his cup was filled he began again. "I remember his dad, Mr. Haughn. He was a Civil War veteran. His name was William Miller Haughn. Everyone called him Bill. Fought at Pea Ridge in the winter of 1862. Heard him tell about the freezing weather and snow on the ground. Said he stood behind a tree and aimed his rifle at the southern boys. He said if he hadn't been a squirrel hunter, he might have been shot. Everyone knows we hide from the squirrel by standing behind a tree. Said he told the soldiers with him to hide behind a tree when taking aim and not to just stand up in the open. If they can see you, they'll shoot you," he told em'."

Gramps laughed and walked to the fire. He lifted the big coffee pot with one hand and filled his cup again. Sitting back down on the ground and leaning against the wagon wheel, he withdrew a long, slim cigar from his shirt pocket. Pressing his thumb nail across the tip of a match, he watched it explode then he held the flame to the cigar. He breathed in and out, puffing loudly as fire showed and smoke hung over his head. He 'enjoyed a good smoke,' he often said.

The expensive cigars came from a company in Florida that he had long done business with and were mailed to the Haughn farm in his name.

Observing the men looking at him, he continued "Mr. Haughn was a big man. Big boned and heavy. Must of weighed two hundred seventy pounds, maybe eighty. He would lead his horse to a stump or a big rock. He'd step upon it, grab a handful of the horse's mane, and take hold of the saddle horn with the other hand. Then with his foot in the stirrup, he'd swing up in the saddle." Gramps' hands raised, lowered, and jerked sideways, imitating the moves he had just described. When he finished talking, he lowered them back in his lap. "I've seen the poor animal lean to one side before he sat down in the saddle." He puffed his cigar thoughtfully then looked at Harlen. "You was just a little boy when your grandpa died. You might not remember him."

"I was six years old when he died. I don't remember much about him."

"Had a heart attack," Gramps continued. "It took a big casket to hold his body, and it wouldn't fit through the doorway. A window had to be removed, and the casket was brought in the house through the opening. It was taken back out through the same opening.

"The rifle he carried in the War rested on nails driven into the wall of the screened in ell porch, next to the kitchen. It had a long barrel – Springfield I believe they called it. It was a one-shot muzzle loader." Gramps turned his cup upside down and shook it to get the last of the dregs out.

Wyatt lay on the ground, his head resting on Skinner's leg. He was lulled to sleep by the sound of Gramp's voice, which was mellow and rich as he sounded each word with the proper emphasis it called for.

Lucas, in his quiet and thoughtful voice, asked another question hoping for an answer. "Do you think the cattle know where they're going and what's going to happen to them. Do any of you have any ideas?"

Lucas searched the faces of each man, and after a lengthy silence, Gramps hoped to satisfy the young boy's curiosity by quoting from the Bible. "The Bible says, somewhere in it, that we're not to question where our food comes from. The hundred and fourth Psalm, verse twenty says: 'When thou makest darkness and it is night, all the beasts of the forest come forth; the young lions roar for prey, seeking their food from God.' All our food comes from God. He provides it all in one form or other." It was quiet for a few moments while each man weighed the words from the Bible. "I don't expect all of them will end up in a skillet on the stove," he concluded, while watching the expression on Lucas' young face.

"I'll tell you one thing," Claude said which surprised everyone because he seldom said a word. "I've been riding behind, eating dust, avoiding cow piles, and bringing up the rear. I've noticed a young bull who won't stay in the herd. He's off to the side or heading toward the front. For two days now I've looked at their rear ends, and I've watched that young bull, who I'll call Casanova, mount every animal. It didn't matter which kind." He laughed and shook his head. "By the time we get to the sale barn, there won't be a virgin in the herd." He slapped his leg, leaned back, and bellowed a loud laugh.

They all watched Claude in his moment of mirth then joined him in laughter.

"At least you have something to look at," Price said. "The only thing we see is open fields, if that makes you feel better."

Silence drifted over the campfire and one by one, the tired field hands - cowboys as of late - began to gather up their bedrolls and drop them on the ground. Some headed to the creek, dropped their clothes on the bank, and jumped in.

Harlen glanced up and saw Skinner trying to shake Wyatt awake, but he seemed too sleepy to respond. Then he tried to pick him up. "Here, let me help you," he said hurrying to his side. They lifted him above the side of the wagon and laid the sleeping boy on the wagon bed. Then Skinner climbed up and into the wagon.

Harlen stepped back from the wagon, and after a moment said, "Men," then raising his voice so he could be heard, continued. "In two more days, and I'm hoping about noon on that second day, we should reach the sale barn, meet the buyer, and leave the cattle there."

He watched Utah scatter and cover with dirt the few coals that remained, pouring water over all, then disappear into the darkness to relieve himself. Harlen tossed his bedroll on the ground by Old Don, waiting for Utah's return. When he did step into the brightness of the lantern, he picked it up and walked to the creek. Setting the lantern on the bank, he undressed and waded into the cool water. Lowering himself until he was completely wet and rubbing a cake of soap across his body, he washed off all the dust, dirt, and sweat that had accumulated over the last two hot days.

Cicadas sang late into the darkness. No breeze blew across the sleeping men to push aside heat ribbons hovering close to the ground. Horses locked their knees and slept standing up until the heavens began to brighten.

Harlen, Price, and young Lucas were drinking coffee and watching the sunrise when the others began to crawl out of their bedrolls. Grouchy men complained about the noisy cicadas while blowing into their tin cups filled with hot coffee.

"Damn noisy bugs," Claude grumbled.

"Ah, they're supposed to make noise," Tex said with a smile covering his face. "That's what bugs do. They make noise."

"Damn katydids," Claude was more specific.

Harlen rode ahead sometimes walking Old Don. Sometimes the gait changed to a trot.

He was somewhat familiar with the terrain, but he studied the ground carefully, not wanting any animal to end up with a broken leg. All the area they were traveling over was mostly flat, tilting ever so slightly toward the east. Low hills loomed in the distance, but they would not be going that far.

He often looked for the highway when there was an opening through the shrubs and trees. Occasionally, he could see Tanner's pickup.

In places, the trees and underbrush were so thick only a snake or rabbit could get through. But then a few feet away, a sliver of sunlight, having found its way through the thick canopy, would light up deep shade. But there were other areas in which only a determined bear could push his way through. He recognized most of the trees: the sycamore, oak, pine, cedar and one the French speaking people called bois d'arc and the natives called bodark. Indians liked the yellow wood of the tree and made bows and war clubs from it. Harlen wondered whether or not the wolves could traverse the underbrush.

As the men followed the cattle, they could see that fall was in the air. Leaves, still clinging to the trees, had begun to take on the colors of yellow, red, and gold.

Each man had his own thoughts as he gazed at the surroundings. At times monotony set in, and one might start wondering if the cattle were leading the men or if the men were leading the cattle? In open spaces with the sky above and relative silence below, one's mind was freed; and, while empty, thoughts crept in of other times and other people who might have crossed that very field.

Gramps could see, in his mind's eye, horses and men running, rifle's firing, and he imagined hearing cannons booming sending grape shot into the flesh of man and animal. He could hear the screams and see the chaos. It called to mind an uncle who was hit by shrapnel and died in the first few days of battle.

Looking down at the ground he half expected to see ruts, mounds of dirt, rifles, blood, and bodies, but he saw only grass and weeds. Soon after the battle ended and the noise stopped, birds, rabbits, and all creatures returned to this field they called home. Gramps turned his head to better hear a cheerful tune from a bird that had flown across the field and landed on a limb in the grove of trees.

He was attuned to God's teachings and remembered a passage from the Bible that said, "He has placed all animals on earth for man's pleasure." In His mercy, he moved them aside to let men wallow in the errors of their ways. Nature and time covered the wounds. Except for the sound of hundreds of hooves stepping, plodding, and prancing, quiet spread across the field.

Tex and Claude lived in the today time. Neither gave much thought to the past, including the Civil War or any war for that matter. They gazed ahead, anticipating a warm welcome in West Plains in a dimly lit upstairs room that sometimes smelled like honeysuckle, other times like roses, but always the sweet, fresh smell of a woman.

Nolan thought about the Civil War in America, which he had read about, and remembered the Revolution in the South American country where he was born and had fled. He counted himself lucky to have avoided both battles.

Skinner and Wyatt looked at the leaves that were changing color but still clinging to the limbs, and they talked about Halloween and Thanksgiving, roasted turkey and pumpkin pies. They laughed at the Halloween prank of tipping over outhouses. As the questions from irate homeowners demanded answers for that awful deed, which occurred yearly, they were half bluffing and didn't expect an answer. No one would ever admit to having done such a thing, though there were a dozen or more young boys and teenagers who only smiled when asked.

Lucas, born fifty years too late to take part in the cattle drives over the Chisholm Trail, imagined being there. He didn't notice the coloring of the leaves as he rode across the fields, for he was looking down the long road in south Texas. He could smell dust stirred up by thousands of longhorns as they trod the dry land and dust mixed with the smell of saddle leather and sweat from his horse filled his nostrils. He could hear the roar of hooves on the wooden bridge that stretched across the Brazos where thousands of longhorns crossed near the twenty year old town of Waco built on the grounds where an Indian village by the same name once stood. They trod the flat prairie land on their way to Kansas, feeding on mesquite shrubs and other grasses that grew in the dry country.

Price, of a serious demeaner - though he enjoyed a good laugh - had sharp eyes and good manners. He liked Harlen and quietly offered him suggestions. His family was in the banking business in Utica, New York, and it was expected he would take part in the family business. Educated in banking and law, though he detested sitting at a desk in a closed-in room, he fulfilled his obligation to his father to whom banking was the only goal to be achieved.

He had other troubles, too. His fiancée could imagine no other life than being the wife of a banker whose family owned the bank. He was unhappy with his job and what his future looked like. He wanted to breathe fresh air in the country with its wide open vistas, not the stale air of his closed-in office. One morning, staring out the window still in his night clothes watching the sun rise, he just couldn't face another day sitting at his desk. By mid-morning, he was still at the window methodically planning the activities for that day.

He wanted to visit his mother and tell her of his plans. After making sure his father had left for the First Merchant's Bank, he walked to the bus stop and waited.

He found her sitting by the window sipping coffee, while overlooking the south side of town. Aware of her son's increasing unhappiness and observing the tension that sometimes surfaced when his fiancee talked glowingly about the bank, she knew this time would come. They talked awhile. Then she kissed his cheek and wished him well.

With his banking days over, he broke off his engagement, resigned his job over the objections of his father, and closed out his bank account. In the early evening with suitcase in hand, he boarded a train to Little Rock, Arkansas. He felt that was far enough away from the east coast, yet close enough to the west, should he decide to go where cowboys lived and worked on ranches, where windblown tumbleweeds rolled across the open land and where millions of stars filled the sky.

Price arrived at the Haughn farm when Harlen was ten years old. He quickly learned to ride and loved being outside breathing fresh air, planting, and harvesting. Soon he decided to stay.

Now following the cattle across that stretch of land, his thoughts began to wander. Glancing skyward, he saw a hawk circling and diving, trying to shake off three small birds who were chasing it away from their nests.

In school he had read about the Louisiana Purchase and Manifest Destiny. But as time drifted by, he began to have doubts of their promises. A longing filled his chest to find out for himself if the history books were right. He looked down at the ground and studied the clods of dirt, the weeds, and the rocks. Opening the history books in his mind once again, he recalled some words which reminded him that, at that very moment, he was moving through part of the Louisiana Purchase. Looking west and north, he could see the beginning of the vast prairie land which once was filled with buffalo. He was riding across the hunting grounds of an Indian tribe called Osage. He was not prepared, as yet, to head west to fulfill the Manifest Destiny Charter.

Harlen knew the land, knew who it belonged to, but kept his eyes on the bull calf and the two baby cows. He judged them to be about three months old, for they could eat hay and grass when the other animals let them. Some of the animals butted and pushed them away from the choice grass. Harlen and Price kept grain in a bucket. They would lure them away from the herd and let them eat from the bucket.

The next to the last field they would cross presented problems of several kind. It hadn't been put to graze nor had it seen a mowing machine in two or three years. It was overgrown with high weeds - some in tassel and prickly burrs - which stuck to everything that touched them and were the devil to get off. Poison sumac bloomed along the edges of the field and berry vines grew in clusters.

Prickly pear cactus grew here and there, and when Gramps saw the plant, he would dismount, pick off the apples that grew on it, blow off the dust, and put one in his mouth. Others he put in his shirt pocket.

Harlen walked Old Don. He discovered low places, large rocks, and saplings half as tall as trees. "Slow the cattle to a walk," he said to Price as their horses walked side by side. "There's poison sumac over there." He stretched an arm in that direction. "Tell the men to walk their mounts and watch out for rocks and thorny vines and berry bushes. I'm going to catch up with Skinner and help him get the wagon across this field."

At least someone, at some point in time, had begun to clean up the field, for rocks had been picked up and pitched, one on top of the other, building a good-sized pile.

It was slow going for animals and men. At times a small cow or bull seemed to disappear, after stepping in a low place with green weeds and brown weeds and bushes growing taller than they were.

The three skinny little calves, that had been abandoned by their mothers and put in the herd because no one wanted them, had a difficult time weaving in and out of the dense vegetation. They often stopped in utter confusion, not knowing what to do. Harlen and Price kept an eye on them, felt sorry for them, and did their best to look after them.

Rabbits darted this way and that trying to get away from hooves. Birds took to the air, frightening the animals who were close to them.

The day was hot and dusty without a breeze, and not even the smallest cloud hung in the sky. Flying insects stuck to wet skin. Stinging sweat burned eyes and trickled down backs, and all shirts were wet with perspiration.

At the edge of the field, which Harlen guessed to be about five hundred acres, was a line of trees. One tree with orange colored fruit stood a short way from the others. Harlen knew it to be a persimmon tree. Over the course of the morning, he noticed Claude riding to that tree and saw him pick two or three from a limb.

There was no water in the field and occasionally a man dismounted, poured water in his hat - sometimes in his hand - and let his horse drink. Afterwards, the canteen was raised to their own mouths. Dust, pollen, buzzing insects, wasps, and whatever else rode the air current prompted the men to reach for the handkerchiefs tied around their necks and pull them over their noses.

After hours of slow but steady travel, they left the overgrown field behind and came upon knee high grass without the underbrush. The cattle stopped to graze, some lying down to rest. While they rested, so did the cowboys, who dismounted and stretched out on the ground.

In late evening gathered around the campfire, the men talked and laughed about having to sleep on the ground in their bedroll in an open field with both flying and crawling bugs.

"Better bugs than snakes," Nolan said. "Did I ever tell you about the time I lived in Wyoming and signed on to a cattle drive that got bogged down by rain in the Sweet Water Valley? So much rain fell that snakes were floating everywhere and..."

"Yes. We've heard that story many, many times," several voices answered.

"I'd give a day's pay, right about now, for a feather bed and a feather pillow," Gramps said.

Harlen pushed his dark brown felt hat back from his forehead and leaned against one of the wagon wheels. "In the fields we've traveled across, I've not seen a man or woman, cow, horse or dog. I'm sure they've seen us for we've certainly made enough noise."

"You're right. I ain't seen a soul of any kind," Utah said, shaking his head for emphasis. "I've been an outrider, staying away from the herd and chasing after runaways. I've been closer to their houses and barns than any of you. Ain't seen a soul."

Claude was known for playing jokes on unsuspecting people. Holding a persimmon in his outstretched hand, he walked over to Lucas who was leaning against Skinner's wagon. "Lucas, did you ever eat a persimmon?" he asked while holding it up for him to see.

"No. I don't believe so," he replied and reached for it. He looked it over then bit into the unripe fruit. With closed eyes and a frown on his face at the tartness, his face muscles froze for a few seconds. He threw the persimmon on the ground.

There were a few low chuckles and smiles all around because each man knew exactly what effect an unripe persimmon had on the taste buds and face muscles.

Lucas grunted and groaned until his face unfroze. He blinked, spat, and spluttered. Instantly anger exploded, and he made a fist and jabbed it onto Claude's chin, sending him staggering backwards and falling on the ground. Claude got up quickly and glared at Lucas who held up another fist and glared back.

"You son of a ...," he glanced at Wyatt then clamped his mouth shut.

"I guess I deserved that," Claude mumbled. "No harm. No harm." He turned and walked away.

Harlen broke the stunned silence by getting up quickly. Holding out his cup he asked, "Price, you got any more coffee in that pot?"

"The pot's half full," he replied pouring into several cups that were quickly pushed forward.

The last fence was in sight. A branch of a minor river flowed through the field, but in this late summer, it was bone dry. Tomorrow, before they reached the sale barn, there would be fresh flowing water for the animals to drink. But tonight, they would bed down with a dry mouth on dry land.

7

A MUCH TRAVELED LAND

Holding his tin cup, Harlen stepped away from the fire and walked a short distance among the cattle, stroking their backs and sometimes pushing one or two aside from where he wanted to walk. He stood gazing at the tree line, and in the last few rays of sunshine that filtered down through the branches, he saw something moving in the trees. He knew it was the wolves – still stalking – still waiting.

"I'll be damned!!" he said out loud and sipped his coffee. He decided to say nothing to the men. They knew they were out there, somewhere.

On this last night, as Harlen's head rested lightly on his saddle, it was filled with the activities of the last three days, and it took a while to fall asleep. Old Don grazed close by and when he had his fill, he walked slowly to where Harlen lay.

Young boy and young colt grew up together. At first, when he was away from home overnight, sleeping on the ground fully clothed and with boots on, he would tie the bridle around his foot. One or two jerks would bring him wide awake. The horse was trained to watch over him until he awakened. Later, Harlen just dropped the reins, and Old Don knew he was to stay where he was.

The wind picked up during the night blowing dust and anything else that was loose. With the change in weather, the cattle became restless.

It was first light when Harlen was aroused from his sleep by the roar of the wind and the milling around of the cattle. Some of the men were still sleeping, while others were stumbling about yawning and rubbing their eyes.

Price was awake and had splashed his face and hands with water poured from a large bucket. He filled the coffee pot and was hovering over a fire trying to make coffee. "Some of you men come over here and stand around the fire," he said without looking up. "Block it from the wind while I put in the grounds."

Three or four walked close to the fire. Some held out their hands to catch the warmth from the sputtering flames. No words were spoken until, at length, the coffee was poured.

Harlen, aware of the wind, dust, and other flying objects and the restlessness of the cattle, said to Price. "I think there's no use in trying to cook breakfast. Slice open a biscuit and put a slab of ham in it. Pass them out to the men, along with a cup of coffee, and let's get on our way."

Standing in a circle eating their skimpy breakfast, knowing on this day they would be free of the cattle, two or three of them had already made plans and were looking forward to a night in town. Some were smiling at the very thought of it.

"This is Saturday, Men," Harlen said. "Before this day is over, the cattle will be at the sale barn!"

"Our job will soon be completed, and we can head back home," Claude said hopefully.

"Not yet," Tex spoke up. "I've got business in town and I know where to find a soft bed."

"Lucas and I are going to hunt down a pair of gloves or two when we get to town." Price informed everyone and glanced at the young man.

The large coffee pot was soon empty, all necessary chores attended to, and the fire covered with dirt until all smoke was extinguished. Cattle milled around, bellowing and butting each other as if irritated. Even the horses were nervous. With their feet in the stirrups, the cowboys mounted their horses, and for the second time, pulled their handkerchiefs over their noses.

Harlen and Price raced after a couple of young bulls that were spooked by flying objects and had run away from the herd. Riding toward the timber line, they spotted the wolf pack. The two young bulls were between them and the wolves and had stopped to graze, unaware of either man or wolf.

With his nose to the wind, the cunning lead wolf picked up the scent of animal and man. Each member of the pack began running, slowly at first, but were leaving the woods behind and gaining ground. The big wolf was the General, and the female and young ones were his Lieutenants. All were trained in stalking and slinking, like hardened battle-ready soldiers.

Harlen fired three shots into the air, and every cow and bull - large and small - began running. The two young bulls ran in opposite directions splitting the wolf pack. Harlen spurred Old

Don and raced after one. Price spurred his palomino and raced after the other, both men firing pistols as they went.

The pack soon forgot about the lone bulls and headed toward the herd.

"It's the wolves," Claude yelled riding hard, trying to head off a stampede as the cattle, spooked by the pistol shots, broke into a run.

"Here they come," Gramps yelled.

The two young bulls were herded toward the others with Harlen and Price at their heels trying to outrun the wolves.

When the cattle caught the wild scent, their eyes glared in fear. They bawled, bucked, and ran. Soon every skittish cow and bull in the herd was bellowing, bucking, and running first in one direction then the other. The cowboys, guns drawn, kept a wary eye on the wolves while trying to keep control of the cattle. Bridle reins were pulled tighter when the horses began quick-stepping and dancing.

Man and animal waited for the attack, and when it came, the big grey led the others into the herd. Snapping, biting, jumping, and snarling. Cattle headed in all directions. The cowboys raced after the bovines trying to turn them in another direction, while shooting at the wolves who were running with the cattle.

One jumped on the neck of a young bull and began biting and slashing with his teeth. The frightened animal shook his head, kicked, bucked, and soon shook him off.

"Shoot the wolves," Harlen yelled. "Don't let them get ahold of the nose." He exchanged his pistol for a rifle, but it was hard to get an aim on the fast-moving melee.

Cows, calves, horses, cowboys, and wolves, set off a din of noise with gunfire, mooing, bawling, yelling, and, an occasional neighing of a wild-eyed horse which had lowered its head to meet its enemy head on, if necessary.

Old Don galloped past the grey stallion, and Harlen noticed Lucas trying to reign in the animal who was rearing, bucking, and turning circles. Suddenly he stopped and remained motionless for a split second, then jumped straight up in the air. When the hooves touched the ground again, the grey headed away from the noise in a dead run. Lucas' only chance to stay in the saddle was to flex every muscle and hold on. Harlen watched them disappear behind the tall trees.

Kicking Old Don in the flanks, he raced to overtake the lead wolf. Aiming his rifle at the large head, he delayed squeezing the trigger to admire the heavy shiny coat and thick fluffy tail held straight out behind. Just before the wolf jumped on a yearling, Harlen squeezed the trigger. It stumbled, ran a couple of steps, then plopped down in death.

A young male wolf nipped at the hind legs of Claude's horse and swung on its long tail. The horse stopped suddenly jerking Claude's body forward and lifting him out of the saddle. He grabbed the horn and hung on when his horse began bucking. Hearing growling from behind him, he turned his head in time to see his horse kick the wolf away sending it flying through the air.

It landed against the breast of Price's palomino, then fell on the ground. The palomino started bucking, bringing its front legs down stiffly time and time again, stomping to death the young canine. The horse leaped over the dead wolf and ran to catch up with the cattle. All the while, the saddle was empty for Price's weight was on the stirrups where his body could better withstand the jarring of the bucking.

Cows and bulls followed their leader, who ran from the wolves at break-neck speed while cowboys spurred their horses to out-run them. After some two or three miles, they began to turn them in a running circle.

One of the young doges set up a loud cry, and Harlen turned to see it being dragged by a large wolf who had sunk its teeth into its nose. The small calf fell head first with blood spurting out its nose. The wolf released its hold and stumbled backwards when a bullet made an opening in its head.

Two pups raced toward the calf, noses in the air, following the scent of fresh blood. Gramps leaned over his saddle, fired his rifle, and one pup stumbled then lay still. The second pup was shot in mid-air. Gramps didn't see the shooter.

Harlen stared at the injured animal and wondered what to do with it. The calf got to its feet, shaking all over. A thin, steady flow of blood ran from its nose.

Skinner Galloway and his ten-year-old son Wyatt had re-packed the wagon and had just settled onto the seat. Wooden boxes placed on the bed of the wagon were packed with food, water, and other supplies for their trip across the Missouri border to West Plains then back home into Arkansas. He laid the leather to the mules to get away as quickly as possible from the noisy skir-mishing. The team's muscles rippled from the strain of the load.

Pulling back on the reins and slowing to a trot, he guided the mules out of the middle of the dust-filled confusion and headed to the side and out of the way of horse or cow. He was looking straight ahead, concerned with the safety of his mules and did not notice the female wolf running behind the wagon.

With a running jump, she landed in the wagon. Her toe-nails scratched the wooden planks as she struggled for balance.

Smelling fresh meat, she headed for the box which contained it, pawing at the lid with both feet.

Skinner felt her weight when she landed and turned to look. Somehow the mules sensed her presence and quickened their gait to a full run.

"Take the reins," he shouted and shoved them into Wyatt's small hands then climbed over the seat. He kicked at the wolf but missed, and with her nose, she raised the lid and her teeth clamped down on a rolled-up paper containing a slab of salt bacon. He slapped at her with a gloved hand.

With the paper in her mouth, she froze and growled. He slapped at her again, and she dropped the bacon and lunged at his hand. He tried to jerk it away, but her conical pointed canines clamped down, penetrating the leather and pulling it half off while blood began to fill the glove and squirt out through the holes.

Lucas, having gained control of his stallion, was galloping at full speed toward the herd and was close to Skinner's wagon when he saw the wolf jump in it. With rifle in hand Lucas aimed quickly and squeezed the trigger. The wolf released her hold and stumbled backwards falling out of the wagon and onto the ground.

Skinner looked up and saw Lucas holding his rifle with smoke curling out the barrel. Then Lucas turned his stallion and raced to the side of one of the mules and grabbed the harness. The team slowed. He looked at Wyatt who was stretched out full length trying to reach the brake with his small foot but failing by inches to do so. His back was against the seat, pulling on the reins with every muscle taut, with a look on his face that said he was about to cry.

"Are you okay?" he asked.

Wyatt nodded yes.

In the distance Harlen noticed a horse and rider racing toward them. At its approach, the horse's hind legs skidded to a stop. The tall man in the saddle held a rifle.

"I'm Clete Jonas," he said. "This is my field, and I was wondering what all the shooting was about." He looked at the dead wolves lying around. "Now I see. I thought all the wolves had been wiped out."

"That's what the newspaper said," Harlen shook his head. "Must of missed a few."

"Are you Harlen Haughn?"

"Yes. I am. We had our hands full there for a little while," he replied. "We don't have time to skin the wolves. You can have the pelts. I don't have time to talk. You can go with me if you want to," and he turned away.

"Is there anything I can do?" Clete Jonas called after him.

Harlen jerked the bridle reins and Old Don turned around. "Yes. There is," he said. "Come with me."

Harlen led him to the injured calf who was still shaking and standing where he left it. They observed a fast drip of blood from its torn nose.

"This calf's nose is torn out by fangs, and I don't want to kill it. Can you take it, keep it, and doctor it? If you can, you can have it."

Clete Jonas got off his horse and looked closely at the wounds. "This is a nice little female Jersey calf. I have Jersey cows myself. I have a milking operation and sell milk to the co-op. Yes. I'll take it," he said while looking up at Harlen. "I'll doctor it and put it on a bottle until the nose heals. It can grow up with my herd. Help me get it on my horse, and I'll take it home."

Harlen stepped down to the ground, and both men picked up the calf. Clete climbed up to his saddle. He reached down and Harlen reached up, and together they were able to get it upon the horse, belly down, with its legs stretched across both sides of the saddle.

"I've got two more skinny little doges you can have if you want them – for free," Harlen said.

They rode among the cattle until they came upon them huddled together shaking like a leaf in a strong wind.

"They're white face," Harlen said and looked at Clete to see whether or not he wanted them.

"Herefords are good milk cows too. If I can get them home, I'll take them."

"Got a couple of ropes?" Harlen asked.

"Yes. I do. I'll lead them home." And he threw the ropes around their necks and tugged gently on each one. The calves moved with the rope.

Clete Jonas rode his horse across the field in a fast walk. Draped across his saddle, still trembling, the little injured calf rested while blood from its nose ran down the side of the horse and dropped on the ground. The other two orphans trotted along behind.

Noticing the wagon had stopped, Harlen raced to see why. Price caught up with him as he reached it.

The fair-haired, sixteen-year-old Lucas bent over Skinner who was sitting on the wagon bed. Gently he pulled on the glove, and when it was free of all fingers, blood poured out of it.

"I heard a shot. What happened?" Harlen asked.

Skinner pointed to the wolf lying close to the wagon. "That female jumped in the wagon and was after our food," he said. "I kicked and hit at her with my hand and she jumped me. Bit my hand." Through it all, his teeth still clamped the stem of his pipe.

Lucas grasped the dipper and scooped it full of water from the barrel which sat inside the wagon, strapped down and fastened to the sides. He poured it across the torn skin, but the deep holes soon filled with blood. He looked at Skinner and said, "You probably need some stiches."

Harlen looked at the hand and knew pain would soon set in. "You need to let a doctor look at that hand," he said. "It looks pretty bad, and we don't have much more than a white rag to tie around it."

From under the wagon seat, Harlen pulled out the box that Laura had packed containing clean cloths and a role of tape. Handing the bag to Lucas he said, "Reach inside and get something to wrap around his hand. There's tape in there also."

He then turned to Skinner. "We'll flag down Tanner in his pickup, and he can take you to a doctor in West Plains. We'll meet you there." Turning to look at his men he asked, "Where's Tex?"

Tex was standing by the mules. "Here I am, Boss," he said walking up to him.

Harlen looked around again and asked, "Where's Claude?"

"Right here, Boss," he answered and stepped close.

"Claude, I want you to help Wyatt drive the wagon. Tex, I want you to help Skinner on Claude's horse and go with him to the highway and flag down Tanner Sullivan in his pickup. Tell him to hurry to West Plains and find a doctor to take care of Skinner's hand." Then reaching inside his leather vest, he pulled out his wallet, opened it, counted out forty dollars, and handed the money to Skinner. "If the doctor needs more, tell him we'll pay up when we get to town."

Skinner turned to Wyatt. "Son I don't know what to say. My hand is tore up pretty bad, and I do need to see a doctor. You've got a good head on your shoulders and you're brave." Removing his pipe with his other hand, he tried to smile. "You're a pretty fair driver, too. Stay with the men. They'll look after you, and we'll meet up in West Plains." Putting the stem of his pipe back between his teeth, he draped an arm across Wyatt's shoulders. The young boy looked up at his father, and their eyes met. "I'm proud of you, Son. You'll do fine." Wyatt's lips trembled but he said nothing.

Tex held the reins while Skinner settled in the saddle. Then he stepped into the stirrup of his own mount.

"We may be moving on toward the sale barn," Harlen said. "You'll have to catch up with us."

Skinner held his arm up, out, and away from his body as they left in a gallop, their horses kicking up small clods of dirt.

Harlen and Price went back to the herd, and Nolan met them. "Did you count them Nolan?" Harlen asked.

"They're all there."

The mustached cowboy's chest rose and fell with heavy breathing from sitting in the saddle, balancing side-to-side for the past three hours. His horse matched wits with strong, stubborn yearlings who resisted returning to the herd. The small horse chomped on the bit while flinging his head up and down spraying the air with foam from its mouth.

Scent from the feral wolves lingered in the air. The restless cattle wanted to run away from the dead canines that were strewn around on the ground. They walked slowly, refusing to stop completely while ignoring the horse and cowboy at their side. Two or three cowboys sat in their saddles, following the cattle and riding away from those who were standing on the ground holding the reins of their horses.

All of them, including Harlen, were more than a little unnerved by the vicious attack and the shooting of the wolves. Their backs were turned away from the bloody scene.

Harlen appreciated Price who stood close by. "I feel half sick. My stomach's turning over and over," he said in a low voice. "I think I might be hungry, or I think I might puke."

Price understood. "Let's just stay right here for a few minutes and do some planning. It's ten o'clock and we might all be hungry, but we can't cook and eat here."

Harlen walked a few steps away sucking in air and pushing it out through his open mouth. After a few moments, he returned to where Price was standing.

"There's one more fence to cut, then there's water on the other side. Let's head the cattle to water, and while they drink, we can eat." They approached the men and told them the plan.

"Let's make tracks!" Harlen called. Men, horses, cows, bulls and wagon continued in a northerly direction.

Price and Lucas cut and opened the last fence, then stood watching seventy-one head of cattle, plus horses and cowboys, pass through. They refastened the fence then let out a yell and laughed heartily. Seating themselves in the saddle, they raced to catch up with the rest.

Cows and horses stood in the water drinking noisily. Utah picked out a place to stop and eat. With head down, he walked around gathering sticks for his fire.

Price joined him by the fire, and they waited for Claude to bring up the wagon. When he arrived, they busied themselves cooking a hearty breakfast which was only a few hours late. Price filled the coffee pot, measured in the grounds, then set it in the coals.

Harlen looked up at the deep blue, cloudless sky. The sun leaned a little past high noon. He guessed the hour was pretty close to one. Two at the latest. His thoughts turned to the sale barn. His dad did not say exactly what time they were supposed to arrive there. He just said 'Saturday'.

Utah took it upon himself to see that Wyatt had a plate full of food, since his father was not there to look after him. Then he sat down beside the young boy while eating.

Harlen was in line behind Gramps who was waiting to fill his plate with hot food. When he put the last spoonful of beans on it, he walked to the wagon and sat down on the ground with his back to the front wheel. Harlen filled his plate, turned to follow, and sat down beside him.

"How are you, Gramps?" he asked, genuinely concerned. Total chaos took over the herd when the wolves attacked, and for about an hour or so, everyone was on his own.

"I'm fine," he replied. "I shot a pup who was chasing a young calf. Bout to catch it, too. How many was in that pack? Looked like a whole bunch to me."

"I counted seven," Harlen replied. "It made for a pretty exciting day with cattle and wolves running everywhere."

They sat in silence while eating then washed the food down with coffee.

Finally, Harlen said, "I hated to have to shoot the wolves but they were bent on killing some of our animals: the young ones, the old ones, or any they could cut from the herd and bring down. I hated, also, to leave the pelts, for they would have brought a few dollars."

Gramps grunted and dug at his food.

"It's a damn shame about Skinner's hand," Harlen said and shook his head. "Hope he doesn't lose the use of it."

Everyone was through eating when Tex came galloping in, holding the reins of Claude's horse. He was greeted and questioned regarding Skinner.

"Did you catch up with Tanner?" Harlen asked.

"Yes. I did. We put another wrap around Skinner's hand. It was bleeding pretty bad. Tanner had a first-aid kit in the glove compartment of his pickup," Tex explained. "Then we put him in the cab, and Tanner lit out with wheels spinnin' and gravel flyin'."

Claude claimed his horse, led him to water, then poured grain on the ground, and stood beside him while he ate.

Price handed Tex a plate he had filled and kept warm. He took the plate, smiled, and said, 'Thank you.' He walked to a tree and leaned against the trunk. Little time was wasted in devouring its contents, and between mouthfuls, he talked about riding to the highway and flagging down Tanner.

"Tanner said he heard a lot of shootin' and saw horses runnin' and wondered what was going on. He said he seen us riding toward the highway so he parked under a nearby tree and waited."

"I filled him in."

The men talked among themselves expressing relief that Skinner was on his way to see a doctor.

When they had finished eating and stood sipping the last of the coffee, Claude, Tex, and Nolan huddled, mumbling something in a voice so low others could not hear. Price smiled and shook his head when a few snickers escaped.

"How will we know when we get five miles from town?" Nolan asked. "I know where West Plains is. I've been there three or four times. But I've never measured the miles."

"There's a good-size sale barn a little way off the highway. It's always been known as being five miles from town," Price said. "Right now, we're about five miles away from it."

"I think it would be a good idea for me to head on up there, look things over, and let them know we're coming in," Harlen said. "I'll take Price with me. You men keep bringing the cattle forward, and we'll meet you before you get there." Raising his hand for quiet for there was yelling and whooping among the men, he added, "Now listen, when we finally get the cattle there, I want all you men to stay close when we meet up with a man named Waymon Jenkins who is to buy our cattle. I don't know the man. Dad called him a hard nose peckerwood who would be tough to deal with. I might need some backup."

The Baxters – father and sons – were close neighbors of the Haughn farm. They had joined the drive with their fifteen head of cattle. While friendly, they had remained mostly to themselves. Before Harlen left, they approached him with their concerns.

"Uh, Harlen, we would like you to talk to the buyer for us if you would," the older man said. "We're not very good at talkin'." and he looked down at the ground. "Just put our cattle in with yours, and when they sell, pay us what we're due," he lifted his head and added, "We would be obliged if you would do that."

"I will do that, Mr. Baxter."

Harlen and Price galloped north, happy that this cattle drive would soon be over and they could go back to cutting hay, if there was any left to cut.

When the sale barn was in sight, the happy look on their faces turned to questions and worries for the place looked deserted. They rode on in, opened the gate, and called out "Hello." They called again, three or four times, when finally a man appeared from behind a gate.

"I'm looking for Waymon. Are you Waymon?" Harlen asked.

"No. I'm not. He's not here. Who are you?"

"I'm Harlen Haughn. He and my dad signed a contract to buy the cattle I'm driving in. They'll be up here in two or three hours."

"Well... Waymon's in Springfield. Left just after noon. He said he was expecting Mr. Haughn and the cattle but guessed they weren't coming, and he had to leave."

Harlen's stomach turned upside down.

"We would have been here sooner, but we ran into a little trouble which delayed us," he explained without going into detail. "When will Waymon be back?"

"Late Sunday night. He'll be on the 11:30 train. I know about the contract. If you want to, we can put the cattle in the feed lot. We can feed and water'um and keep 'um pinned up. If you want us to do that."

Harlen glanced at the sky then looked off in the distance. His dad's face stared back at him. A hundred questions sped through his mind. The plans he made changed quickly, and just as quickly, he made new ones. He decided to leave the cattle there.

"That'll be okay." His voice held disappointment mixed with a little disgust. "What time will Waymon be here Monday morning?"

"He'll be in about 9:00 o'clock."

"We'll ride out to meet the cattle and bring'em in."

Turning their horses around, they walked slowly out the gate. Neither said anything until the disappointing words settled into their minds. When they did, Harlen spurred Old Don to a gallop.

"Ah, Hell!" he said. "Let's get it over with." Price rode at his side. Soon they rejoined the herd.

They were on the down slope of a hill. Cows, bulls, and horses trotted through the last of the seasonal grass. In the far distance, a group of buildings appeared.

"That must be West Plains," Harlen commented.

"It is, but look over there," Price said and pointed to a low building surrounded by a fence. "That's the sale barn. That's where we came from, and that's where we're going."

The men let out a yell and urged their horses forward. Even the cattle, trotting a little faster, seemed to know the long walk was almost over.

A wide gate was thrown open and the cattle rushed in. There was hay in an open feeder, and near the middle of the fenced-in acreage was a pond. Some began to eat while others headed for the pond.

Tanner drove his car through the gate, stopped, then got out. "What's happening?" he asked

Harlen gathered the men and explained the situation. "We're going to be held over 'till Monday," he said. "The buyer is in Springfield and won't be back to the sale barn until Monday morning. We can't go home 'till we sell the cattle." He searched their faces to see their reaction.

"If any of you really want to go back home, you can. But I need some of you to stay with me." Harlen turned his head to take in the surroundings. "There's no use stayin' around here," he said. "We should probably go on into town. I need to find Skinner."

He looked at Wyatt who was smiling broadly at the mention of his dad's name. "Can I go with you?" he asked Harlen.

"Absolutely you can."

"There's a new motel and café at the edge of town. It'd be a good place to stay," Tanner said. "Skinner's been at the hospital. The doctor made arrangement for him to stay there at no extra charge. He might want to join us at the motel."

"We could all ride in to town," Harlen said. Then he asked Mr. Baxter what he wanted to do and posed the question to the others. "Who wants to go back home? Who wants to stay?"

In a low voice Mr. Baxter talked to his sons, withdrew his wallet, counted the money, then turned to Harlen.

"We'll stay," he said.

"We can't leave the wagon and all the supplies here without someone staying with it." Harlen said. Turning to Tanner he asked, "Do you suppose we could keep it near the motel? Do you think they'd let us?"

"Oh! I'm sure they would," he replied. "There's a lot of open space around there."

In one voice, the others said. "We'll stay."

Tanner asked Harlen if Wyatt could ride to town in the pick-up. Harlen laughed and said "He'd probably get a kick out of that. Ask him."

With wide eyes the young boy waited for Harlen's okay then ran to the pickup, opened the door, and jumped in.

Everyone mounted up.

"We'll follow you to town and the motel," Harlen called to Tanner.

There would be no more open fields covered with grass and other vegetation. The highway was paved with gravel.

8

OFF INTO THE NIGHT

Seven men on horseback, following a wagon pulled by two mules which was following a pickup, was quite a site to see as it rolled on toward West Plains. Twice they pulled off the highway to let three cars and one large truck pass.

When they reached the motel Tanner said he would take Wyatt to see Skinner and suggested they would be back later.

Several cars were parked in front of the building when they rode in. Claude stopped the wagon under a cluster of tall trees a short way from the entrance. All dismounted, and bridle reins were tied to any part of the wagon they could fasten on to.

Price and Lucas led their horses away from the wagon then climbed up in their saddle.

"We're going to town to buy some gloves," Price said. "We should be back before supper time." They put the spurs to the horse's sides, galloping off up the road.

While waiting for the return of those who would be eating supper, the ones left behind stayed close to the wagon, watching men and women go into the restaurant. With keen interest, they observed how the guests were dressed.

They began to take notice of their own clothes. With their hands, they brushed the sleeves and the front of their shirts. Then they swiped the front and back of their pants. Lifting a booted foot, they rubbed the toe against the back of their pant legs.

In late afternoon Price and Lucas returned. Lucas showed his gloves to everyone, trying them on and laughing all the time. While everyone was admiring the gloves, Tanner drove his pickup onto the grounds. He, Skinner, and Wyatt stepped down to the ground.

Harlen rushed over to Skinner, asking about his hand.

Skinner smiled and held up his hand which was covered with a white bandage. "It's coming along just fine."

"When do we eat? Or did I miss supper?" Price asked.

"No. You didn't miss supper, but I think we ought to get cleaned up before we go inside," Harlen suggested. "We could at least get into a clean shirt."

The men moved to the other side of the wagon, the one turned away from the windows of the café, and began searching for clean clothes. Peeling off their dirty and sweaty shirts they exchanged them for slightly wrinkled but clean ones. Dusting off their pants and boots as best they could and combing their hair, they tried to look presentable to the city folks who were inside.

Harlen took a few minutes longer to look presentable. He found a rag in the wagon and rubbed the dust, mud, and manure off his boots. A cold biscuit cooked in lard and rubbed across the leather, put a shine on them.

They went inside the building as a group. The Saturday night dinner crowd turned to look at the cowboys, fresh off their horses. Each man removed his hat and held it in his hand.

"Harlen Haughn is that you?" a voice called out, and the man hurried to shake his hand.

Harlen stared in amazement at Evan Lumsden. "What are you doing up here?" they both asked at the same time. Evan looked at the group and asked if they were all together. Finding that they were, he ushered them into a large, empty back room.

He turned to Harlen. "I just came along for the ride," he said. "What about you?"

"Me and these men drove a herd of cattle to the stockyards here in West Plains," he said.

Evan was with two other men, and introductions were made around the room. To Harlen he said, "I'd like you to meet Carl Ridley and Hayes Perkins from Oklahoma. They're long- time friends of mine."

"Pleased to meet you I'm sure," he replied. Turning to the men he said, "Everyone introduce yourselves to a very good friend of mine - and to his friends."

Hand shakes and introductions took a little time, but finally, thoughts turned to food. "Have you all had supper?" Evan asked.

"I'm sure we're all hungry," Harlen said with a laugh." I know I am."

Carl stepped forward. "I just had this motel and café built. I own this one and several others. That is my line of business. Someone said you were from Elizabeth, Arkansas? I own the café and motel there. Carl's Dad's Café? You may have heard of it."

"I sure have," Harlen replied. "I've eaten there several times."

"Today was our Grand Opening here," Carl said with a wave of his arm and a confident smile. "Oh, do any of you need a room for the night?"

"I'll have to get back to you after I check with the men. I know I want a room."

"Some of our rooms have two beds. Some have just one."

"Harlen, I could use the other bed if we could share a room," Gramps spoke quietly and waited for Harlen's reply.

"Sure, Gramps. No use sleeping on the hard ground when you don't have to," was the welcome reply.

None of the other men wanted a room. "We'll just sleep under the wagon or close by it," some said.

"Wyatt and I will sleep IN the wagon," Skinner said with a smile.

Steaks, chops, chicken and bowls of vegetables and trays of bread laid out on the table began to dwindle and soon disappeared. Glass after glass of water and half a dozen pots of coffee washed the food down.

Claude, Nolan, and Tex left the table, got on their horses, and galloped off into the night heading for the dimly lit upstairs room which had a warm welcome for any man. A short time later, Price's palomino trotted to the road which lead into town.

Gramps, Skinner, Harlen, Evan, Carl, Hayes, and Lucas spent the remainder of the pleasant evening talking. Wyatt dozed off to sleep at the table, and Carl scooted three chairs side-by-side. The boy was laid across them – still sound asleep.

Skinner's hand was wrapped in a thin bandage held together with a safety pin. "It don't hurt much anymore and, I'll have the full use of it," he said. "Doc wants it to stay wrapped up a little longer so it don't get infected."

"Did you have enough money to pay the doctor?" Harlen asked.

"I've got ten dollars left." He reached in his pocket gathered the money and handed it to Harlen.

"Keep it. Just think of it as a bonus."

Skinner stared at him. "Thanks a lot!" He put the bills back in his pocket.

Harlen turned to face Evan. "Evan tell me about your farm and I want to hear about Pearl and the kids."

Instantly a smile appeared on Evan's face as the words tumbled out about everyone and everything on his farm.

Harlen studied Hayes and liked what he saw. "Hayes I've heard about you. I'm guessing you're the one they call Cowboy. Am I right?"

"You sure are. I've been called that and other names," He said with a laugh. "I don't rodeo anymore. I'm the local veterinarian now."

Then Harlen turned to Carl. How many motels do you own?" he asked.

"This is my fourth one," he said. "My next one will be in Springfield. It should open in early summer."

After four intense days and three nights in the open air, it was good to sit at a table where warm pie and hot coffee were within reach. Overhead lights lit up the room, and starched, white curtains hung from the windows.

Conversation and information from close to home was a welcome treat.

The hour grew late, and the evening ended when each person headed for a bed, whether inside or outside.

As the early dawn of Sunday morning approached, the birds began to sing. It was as if it was their sworn duty to awaken everyone who walked on two legs, those who walked on four legs, all that crawled on the ground, and all that took to the air.

To some, however, morning came too soon. For the men who traded sleep for a warm welcome in an upstairs room where they could lie down on a bed of down, much coffee was needed.

Gramps ate two eggs and drank his coffee. He sliced open a biscuit, poured molasses over it and took a bite. A church bell rang, and he stopped chewing and smiled. It had been a long time since he had heard a church bell. Stuffing the last of the biscuit in his mouth, he stood up. "I'm going to try and find that church where the bells are ringing," he said and hurried out the door.

"Say a prayer for me," Harlen called after him.

Gramps threw a blanket on his mare, then a saddle. "We're going to church," he told her. Tightening the cinch under the animal's belly, he patted her on the neck then stepped up into the stirrup and pressed his knees against her.

They trotted down the highway, listening for another ring of the bell. In the distance a small white church stood out in the still green meadow. In back of the building was a thick grove of trees that were beginning to show their new fall colors. The bells sounded sweet to his ears and kept ringing while he approached.

All the church goers were already inside and he could hear the words of a familiar hymn being sung. Four cars were parked at the side, a few wagons sat close by. Several horses were tied to branches of a small tree. Gramps dismounted and wrapped the reins around a low hanging limb.

With closed eyes, he stood by his mare for a moment resting his hand on her neck. The words of the song washed over him, and he turned his face heavenward. Still with closed eyes, his voice joined with the others; "Shall we gather at the river, the beautiful, beautiful river..." then he opened them to see the mare had bent her neck and was looking at him.

He stopped singing. "You don't like my song?" he asked her. She looked away. "Well, I'll take my singing inside, and you can stay out here and listen to the birds."

Once inside, he removed his hat, held it to his chest, and sat down in the nearly empty back row. Again, he joined the singing. "On a hill far away, stood an old rugged cross," and as he sang, the weariness of the trip was forgotten. Something akin to peace invaded his thought pattern and a calm spread over him.

He listened to the words from the Bible that the white-haired preacher was reading to the congregation, then folded his hands in prayer. His eyes were shut tight, and his lips moved in silence as he poured his heart out to the Almighty. With the Amen said, he quietly slipped out the door, untied his mare, and headed back to town.

Earlier in the year when shoots and roots were growing Laura had taken the grubbing hoe and chopped roots from the sassafras tree. She carried them to the cellar where they would dry.

On this Sunday morning, she and Joe had hurried through breakfast, cleaned up the kitchen, and dusted and swept each room, in anticipation of Harlen and the men arriving back home.

In the sunny but cool morning, she gathered a handful of dried roots from the cellar, carried them to the kitchen, washed them, put them in a pot of cold water, then set it on the stove to boil. When the water turned red, she pulled the pot away from the heat, and while it steeped, she gathered cups and saucers. She and Joe sat quietly in their chairs, each one deep in thought. They sipped the hot tea and rocked slowly, while a gentle breeze played with the few yellow leaves that had fallen on the ground.

Joe thought about the cattle and the money they would bring. It was his plan to make an installment to the bank on the two thousand dollar loan he had with them. There was no doubt in his mind about Harlen's ability to carry through with the job that had fallen to him. He sometimes thought his injury had been a blessing - in a way - for it allowed his only son still at home to mature into manhood. It was nearing three weeks since he was injured. His back only bothered him when he bent over too far.

Laura's thoughts were on Harlen and all the men. She hoped the drive had gone well, cattle sold, money in pocket, and all headed home today. She wondered if she had sent enough food with them. She wondered if anyone had been hurt. She wondered and hoped and turned her head to look up the road to see if she could see them riding in. She strained to hear the iron wagon wheels as they rolled over rocks. All was silent. She sipped her tea and waited, as her mother and grandmother sipped their tea and waited - for their child to come home, for fruit in the orchard to ripen, for a baby to be born...

This Sunday was different for all. It was late morning when Gramps returned from church. Harlen was restless as he sat in the motel room. He paced across the floor and stood looking out the window, finally returning to his chair. After a while, he went outside to see what the men were doing.

There was a flurry of activity when a train whistle blew loudly. Tanner asked if anyone wanted to go see the train. "We can go in my pickup," he said.

Wyatt ran to him, "Can my dad and I go?" he asked excitedly. "Sure, you can. Get in."

Soon the vehicle was loaded, in the cab and in the truck bed, as the men jumped in and sat down.

Tanner spent a lot of time in West Plains and knew where the best area for train watching was. Soon they were parked on a curve, as the Springfield-to-Memphis train sped down the track. All stood by the track and watched, but when the train began to curve around a bend in the terrain, Wyatt ran away from the track.

"Move back, Dad, or the train will run over you!" he all but cried. When the big train sped on by, Wyatt stood speechless for a short while. Finally, he said, "That's the biggest thing I've ever seen."

Harlen, Price, and Gramps decided to go for a ride to see the town. Utah was busy with the curry-comb rubbing down one of the mules. "You want to go with us Utah?" Harlen asked.

"No. I'll stay with the wagon," he replied.

"You didn't want to go see the train?"

"No. I've heard about trains. If I saw one, it would probably scare me to death."

Harlen smiled and the three walked their horses to the gravel road.

As they approached the Square in the middle of town - as most towns in mid America were laid out - Gramps recited a little Civil War history. "My uncle was killed here," he said. "A cannon ball burst, spreading shrapnel all around, killing several men who were close by. My uncle was one of them." They were silent for a time sitting astride their horses looking out across the Square as if they could see the raging battle.

"There's a famous baseball player from here," Gramps informed them, lifting his voice on a happier note. "Preacher Roe is his name. He's a left-handed pitcher for the Saint Louis Cardinals. I was in Saint Louis once and got to see one of his games."

They arrived back at the motel in time to say goodbye to Harlen's friend Evan Lumsden and his friends Hayes and Carl. They stood watching as the car headed to the highway. Tanner's pickup did not return until much later.

9

SHADE TREE POKER

The four men, including Utah, sat on the ground while Gramps shuffled the cards. Each had tossed five one-dollar bills into the pot, and the cards were dealt.

The responsibility that had been placed on Harlen's shoulders filled his thoughts. He thought of his dad - the man with a stern face and light blue eyes who expected perfection. He wondered what he was doing and thinking at that moment.

His thoughts turned to his mother who displayed the Victorian manners taught to her by her mother, who, also, was groomed in the Victorian way by her mother. She spoke in a gentle voice and had a ready smile. While his dad oft times used a loud and harsh voice, he found the gentleness of his mother comforting and encouraging, building his confidence to face his dad when he yelled at him. He loved her soft voice and gentle ways. He knew she would be very worried when he did not come home.

Joe's parents had been gone several years, and his siblings scattered off to other states, except two sisters. Laura's parents were also gone, but her siblings stayed close. She and all her brothers and sisters nurtured their close relationship. The closeness was not there among Joe and his siblings. Visits were seldom, each one busy with their own life.

Joe and Laura had seen their two oldest sons marry and leave home, eventually going to California and finding jobs there. They seldom saw their grandchildren.

Harlen had watched his mother through her last three pregnancies. She was one month away from forty-three years old when her last child was born. Her arms, legs, neck, and face were very thin.

He had watched her carry a bucket of corn out to the chickens. She called, "Chick, chick, chick" while all the poultry gathered around her. She scattered the feed on the ground by the handfuls, then stepped inside the chicken house to gather their eggs. If a hen was still on the nest she would slide her hand under her and gather up the eggs, but sometimes the hen would object and peck her hand. Laura would scold her and say, "Now don't do thaaaat."

He watched her closely through the cold of winter, when the wind blew against the bare walls of the house hunting cracks to whistle through. Tending to the outside chores, she pulled her coat around her and pinned it closed with a large safety pin because the buttonholes were stretched wide and the button would slide out.

He had watched her, heavy with child in the hot summer, standing over the stove stirring vegetables, fruit, or jelly with her hair unkept and small children pulling on her dress. He had been uncomfortable looking at her large belly.

When time came for her baby to be born, he would call to mind something she had told him in confidence. "I fear for my very life," she had whispered to him. She then told him, once again, that one of her sisters, and a sister-in-law had died in childbirth.

But Harlen was still at home with his two sisters, one whom he would rather tease than spend time with, and he had little time for the other. He was shy by two weeks from being seventeen when the last child of Joe and Laura – his third sister - was born.

Joe leaned over the bed and looked at the newborn. "She's awful small," he observed.

Harlen didn't trust himself to carry the tiny baby in his arms, so he laid her on a pillow and carried it.

Sitting under the trees on this Sunday, and listening to the chirping of the many bugs who lived in the woods he played his cards, winning one hand, loosing another. He did not hold himself guilty for the circumstances he was in because he had no control over any of it. His mind drifted toward his mother whom he knew would be planning a special dinner – as she always did on Sunday – "for you never know who might come for a visit," she often said.

Laura was planning the menu in her mind for this Sunday dinner as supper time approached. "Joe," she said, "I'll fry up a chicken if you'll go catch that old fat hen."

Without a word, and carrying a stiff wire with a hook on the end he walked through a cluster of white and red chickens.

When he came to that 'old fat hen,' he hooked her by the leg then wrung her neck.

They waited on the veranda until the food began to get cold. Finally, they sat down at the table and ate in silence.

Harlen was awake long before daylight. He anticipated this Monday morning would be a tough one when he met up with 'the old peckerwood,' as his dad called Waymon.

He dressed and walked outside. None of his men were stirring about. The café was open, and waitresses in white starched aprons were busy with a few customers. He could smell coffee so he made his way there. The waitress greeted him with a cheerful, "Good morning. Coffee will be ready in a couple of minutes. Sit down. Do you want breakfast?"

He was on his second cup when Price, Gramps, Nolan, Lucas, Claude and Tex came through the door. The others soon arrived, including Mr. Baxter and his sons. All ordered breakfast. Everyone was in a good mood - even Claude - and they talked, laughed, and ate. The clock on the wall behind the counter chimed seven o'clock.

"When you all finish eating, you need to settle up your account here then get packed and head on down to the sale barn," Harlen said. Taking the last drink from his cup, he added, "I'll be doing the same."

Gramps, Lucas, and the other men were still on their horses, waiting just outside the sale barn when Harlen, Price, and Nolan arrived.

"Let's go see about our cattle," Harlen said and trotted Old Don to that enclosure. All the men followed, for all were anxious to see about them. They dismounted and Harlen went inside the corral, walked among the herd, and, when satisfied as to their welfare, led Old Don to water then started back toward the gate.

"I'm looking for Joe Haughn," a deep throated voice called out. "Have any of you seen him?"

Harlen turned to see a portly man hurrying to catch up with him. The pant legs tucked inside his boots outlined his short bow legs. A holster was buckled around his hips, and the handle of a pistol curved out over its edge. With every step it flopped.

"I'm Harlen Haughn. Joe is my dad."

"I'm Waymon Jenkins," and said and held out his hand and gripped Harlen's.

Price stood by Harlen and could hear everything that was said between him and Waymon. Only if Harlen called upon him would he join in the conversation or offer advice. He listened attentively, keeping quiet.

Waymon stepped back and looked at the young cowboy. It was a long minute before he said anything. He spat a mouth full of tobacco juice on the ground, splattering his boots. Finally, he said, "I had hoped to buy the cattle from Joe. You're pretty young to be selling cattle. Are these cattle from the Haughn Ranch?" Without waiting for an answer, he added, "By chance you didn't pick up any strays along the way, now did you?"

Harlen stiffened and frowned at the suggestion that he might have a few strays mixed in with the herd.

He didn't like the tilt of the man's head, nor did he like the teasing smile on his face. He looked at Waymon from head to toe, noticing his stained shirt and wrinkled pants. Harlen wondered why he didn't dress with a little more care, since he was 'the man out front' who met everyone who came to the sale barn.

"How old are you anyway?" Waymon asked with a loud laugh and looked behind him at several men who joined in the laugh.

Harlen had steeled himself and was not going to let the man goad him into becoming angry. "I reckon it don't matter how old I am," he replied firmly.

"Maybe you're not old enough to legally make a trade. What do you think about that? I need to know your age."

Some of the men on the other side of the fence rode in and bunched around Harlen. Waymon took note of their presence but stood his ground.

"Well," and his gaze dropped to a small rock that he kicked at with his boot, "how do I know these animals are from the Haughn farm? Do they have a brand? I need to see a brand." Up to this point, Waymon had a mocking smile on his lips, but that changed as he took a few steps toward the feed lot.

Harlen dismounted and followed. "The cattle on my farm all have the capital H brand. See for yourself. We also brought in fifteen head without a brand that belongs to a neighbor," he said to Waymon who stopped and glared at him.

"A neighbor huh? You rustled those along the way, did you? Does Joe know you're a cattle thief?"

Gramps and the rest of the cowboys dismounted and hurried to Harlen's side, walking with him to the feed lot. Gramps carried a rifle which rested across his left arm.

Waymon pulled the pistol from his holster and pointed it toward the ground. The men who seemed to be friends of his moved closer.

Harlen frowned and his eyes followed the pistol. He was surprised and wondered why he wore a holster fitted with a gun. He was aware that most men had a pistol or knife on them for self-protection during the lawless days of the boot-leg trade, but he didn't know anyone who carried them in the open. As far as the outlaw days of the Wild West, he knew that bit of history had been settled years ago. He was beginning to wonder what kind of place this was that the man felt a need to strap on a holster. Was he afraid a gang of outlaws would ride in, open all the gates, empty out the corrals, and make off with the cattle?

Waymon leaned over the fence looking at the capital H on each animal's hip, which was burned through the hair by a red-hot branding iron.

The Baxter's stepped to the front of the group. "The fifteen head without a brand is my cattle," the older man said. "We grouped them in with the Haughn herd for this drive up here. They ain't stole neither," he added with a defiant look on his face.

"Well now," Waymon said, putting his pistol back in the holster. He looked at Harlen. His lips parted in a rather crooked smile, which drew down the corners of his mouth making it look like a smirk. He was satisfied that he had bluffed this young green horn. "How many head did you say you had?"

"Seventy-one," Harlen said.

Waymon was dubious. "I'll need to count them."

"By all means. Let's do that."

All the cowboys climbed over the fence and, each one began a count of his own. After a length of time Waymon said, "I count sixty-three." He climbed upon the fence, sat down on the top railing, and rested his elbows on his knees.

"I count seventy-one head of bulls and cows," Harlen said firmly.

"Aw, no. You're wrong," Waymon said in a rising voice. Jumping down from the fence he added, "My count is sixty-three."

A chorus of voices shouted out, "Seventy-one!"

He glared at Harlen while thinking that if he could get away with his count, he could save himself a few dollars. But, glancing at the men who had moved closer to Harlen, he knew they had called his bluff.

Trying to laugh it off, he shrugged and said, "I may have missed a few. Tell you what I'll do. I'll give you five cents a pound for all of them and take them off your hands."

Harlen swung back into the saddle. "I'll take twelve cents a pound for the yearlings and bulls, ten cents a pound for cows, and nothing less." His lips barely moved.

Waymon clapped his hands, leaned back and let out a high pitched laugh while his protruding stomach bounced up and down. He looked at his men and said, "Boys, what do you think of that?" They, too, laughed a loud boisterous laugh.

Harlen shot a glance at Price, Nolan, and then to the others behind him.

When he and his men stopped laughing, he said with a straight face. "I'll give you five cents a pound, and that's my top dollar. Take it or leave it." Turning, he started walking back to the building.

"You backing out of the deal you signed with my dad?" Harlen called after him.

Waymon spun around. "I make deals with grown men. Not little boys."

Anger showed on his red face and he patted the holster that hung loose and low on his stubby leg. Finally, he turned his back and walked on.

"Round up the cattle and head 'em out the gate," Harlen said. His men climbed back in the saddle and kicked their mounts in the flank. They trotted forward.

Waymon was startled. He stopped and held up his arms.

"Wait a minute!" he hollered. "Let's talk this over. Maybe we can come to some kind of agreement."

Harlen was disgusted. "Pay me what I quoted you, and every animal is yours. Otherwise, I'll take 'em back to the farm."

He sat still for a long minute waiting for his answer. When it didn't come, his foot gently touched Old Don, and he took a few steps toward the corral. Lucas had dismounted and opened the gate and a few head were already out.

"Wait a minute!" Waymon hollered again.

Harlen looked at him as he rode past. He could see the man was flustered and swung his arms in confusion.

"Okay! I'll pay your price," he shouted.

The horses and cowboys stopped, but the cattle did not. "Bring 'em back," Harlen shouted.

The cows and a few bulls were herded back into the corral.

Waymon turned around and stalked toward the building. He motioned for Harlen to follow. Harlen dismounted, and with Price, Nolan, and Mr. Baxter behind him, they followed him into his cramped and darkly lit office.

"Sit down," he said and waved his hand at the chairs lined up against the wall.

Waymon jerked a chair away from his desk and bent his knees in preparation to sit down on it. The chair looked so small and fragile the men were sure it would crumble from his weight. Amazingly, it held firm. "Sit down," he mumbled again.

They stared at the half dozen or so chairs. Each one had been upholstered with black and white spotted cow hide with the hair still attached. They slowly sank onto the chairs.

Once their eyes adjusted to the dimness of their surroundings, they were surprised at the neatness of his scarred-up desk. A neat stack of papers and a small jar holding pens and pencils were all that was on it. They wondered at the contrast between the office and his untidy personal appearance.

Waymon cleared his throat, and the conversation began that would transfer ownership of the bovines to him and the sale barn.

But Waymon wanted to harangue the young cowboy some more. "What kind of papers do you have that can convince me you didn't steal this bunch of cattle?"

Harlen's eyes narrowed. "My word has always served me well, at least in honest places I've done business with. I'm beginning to wonder if you're running an honest business."

The smirk that served Waymon as a smile disappeared, and he stiffened.

"Tell you what I'll do," he began and wiped his hands on his shirt. "I'll take all the cattle off your hands, for nothing in exchange, and you and your men can ride on out of here and go back to the farm."

"When you meet my price," Harlen said.

"And mine," Mr. Baxter joined in.

"I don't pay for stolen cattle. Now you and your men head on out of here, or I'll call the sheriff and have you all thrown in jail for cattle rustling."

He fumbled for his gun aiming to lay it on his desk but it fell to the floor. He scooted his chair back and bent over to retrieve it. Upon rising his eyes met a small pistol pointing at his guts.

Waymon grunted loudly and shoved the gun back into his holster. His eyes were fixed on the barrel of Harlen's pistol. "What are you doing?" he almost shouted in surprise.

Harlen was more afraid of the gun in the holster then he would admit, because he was sure Waymon didn't know how to use it. Not knowing how to handle it was far more dangerous than knowing how.

"I'm tired of you threatening me. How does it feel to have a gun drawn on you?"

"Well...Uh...I really wasn't going to shoot," he said with a nervous laugh.

"If you point a gun at someone, you better be willing to use it. If you're just bluffing, you're likely to get shot."

"Well, aw..." He shrugged his shoulders and leaned back in the small fragile chair and looked at Harlen.

"Now then," Harlen spoke slowly and firmly while still pointing his pistol at the short, bow-legged, contrary man who sat behind a desk in a chair that was much too small for the heavy man. "You take out your pen and checkbook and write a check - made out to me - and I will hand over the Bill of Sale and the Contract you and my dad signed, or I'll go get the sheriff and have you arrested for failing to honor these papers." He waved them in the air.

Waymon opened a drawer and brought out a checkbook. He reached for a pen, shook it, looked at it then put his tongue to its tip. "How do you spell your name?"

"H-a-r-l-e-n. The last name is spelled the same as my dad's last name. I guess you know how to spell that."

They glared at each other for a long moment. Before pen touched paper Waymon couldn't resist one last jab.

"It's going to be a lot of money for a kid still wet behind the ears to be carrying around. You up to it?" he snarled.

Harlen laughed outloud, "I'm up to it," he said and slid his pistol back in his boot.

The check was written and handed over. With one hand Harlen reached for the check. With the other he handed over the Bill of Sale and the Contract. Nothing more was said. Placing the check inside his leather vest, they left the office heading for their horses. He mounted Old Don and trotted toward the gate followed by his men.

They left the sale barn heading for the highway but stopped before they reached the road.

"Some of you men need to head home. I've got to go to the bank in West Plains and cash this check to pay Mr. Baxter. Price, you stay with me. Mr. Baxter, you need to come along too." He looked at Skinner. "Take the wagon and head on back. Don't be surprised if you meet Dad coming to see about us." Turning toward them all he said, "We accomplished what we set out to do. Thanks Men." With a wave of his hand, he added, "Now go back down the road and find a place to stop for the night. I've got business at the bank, then I'll join you before supper."

Mr. Baxter had dismounted and motioned for his two sons to follow him. They walked a few steps away from the group.

"You need to go back home," he told them. "I'm sure your momma is worried sick by now. I'll go on to West Plains with Harlen and collect my money, then we'll catch up with the wagon. I'll stay the night with the rest of the men and head home tomorrow."

The boys rode south with the group. Mr. Baxter, Price and Harlen rode north. The five miles back to West Plains was covered in an easy gallop. They rode past the bank and on around the square, then back past the bank. They stopped in a nearby alley and dismounted.

One car and three wagons, with their teams still hitched to them, sat in the tall grass. Several horses were tied to hitching posts. Price and Mr. Baxter added their bridle reins to the small space still available on the posts. Harlen dropped Old Don's reins to the ground.

With their hands, they brushed off their shirt and pants. Then Harlen pulled out a rag that was tied to his bedroll and wiped off his boots.

10

SPURS JINGLING

The three men stepped on to the sidewalk - spurs jingling - and walked the half block to the bank. Pushing open the glass doors, they stepped inside and paused. The floor was covered with small, square, gray-glazed tile. The ceiling was covered with pressed tin. A long narrow window looked out upon the street. Several people waited at the three tellers' windows.

Price and Mr. Baxter remained behind while Harlen got in line. When it was his turn to speak to a teller, he slid the check under the bars that covered the window.

The clerk, dressed in a suit and necktie, took the check, looked at it, then looked at Harlen.

"Are you Harlen Haughn?" he asked.

"I am."

"This is an awful big check for such a young person to be carrying around. Do you think you will be safe with all this money on you?"

The questions and assumptions caught Harlen off guard. His dad had warned him about Waymon. But now, this man seemed to be questioning his integrity, and it touched a sore spot that had arisen at the sale barn. For a moment he was speechless. It was the last straw, as anger rose to the surface.

"Hell's bells," he said in a voice slightly raised and filled with disgust, which caused some of the customers in the bank to turn and look at him. He didn't care. "Just cash the damn check," he said and glared at the teller.

The man in the suit and necktie remained calm, left the window, and entered a room to talk to another man who sat behind a desk. After a few moments, both returned to the window and stared at Harlen.

"What is your name?" the other man asked.

"Harlen Haughn," he answered in a low tone.

"Are you related to Joe Haughn?"

Shifting to the other foot, he stepped back from the window and with hope in his voice answered, "He's my dad."

The man who had sat behind the desk smiled. "Cash this man's check," he told the clerk and hurried to the lobby where Harlen stood. He held out his hand and Harlen slowly reached for it.

"I'm Truman Everson," he smiled. "I'm president of this bank, and I've known your dad for several years. He's a cattleman, and he's done business with this bank for a long time. I'm pleased to meet his son."

Harlen smiled but was taken aback.

"Now how would you like this money? Mr. Haughn always wanted cash. How else can I help you?"

Pointing to Mr. Baxter, he said, "I need to pay this man for his cattle and I'd like you to check my figures."

Mr. Everson glanced at Price and Mr. Baxter. Then he raised his arm, motioning to all of them, "come back to my office and we can handle this from there."

Footsteps were quieted when they stepped on the carpet that lined the hallway. Inside the office they quickly scanned the dark wood walls, carpeted floor, and massive desk, which Harlen stood in front of while watching Mr. Everson press the white keys on the adding machine.

When he finished, he tore off the paper and handed it to Harlen. "This is the amount you owe Mr. Baxter, and your figures are correct. Now you all stay here while I go to the safe and get the money. Do you want cash?"

Harlen nodded yes.

He returned a few minutes later holding a fist full of greenbacks. Counting out the money owed to Mr. Baxter, he reached for a brown envelope and placed the bills inside then handed it to him. Counting out the rest of the money and putting it inside another envelope, he handed it to Harlen.

Both men placed the envelopes in their vest pockets and followed Mr. Everson out of the office. When Harlen passed the teller in the suit and necktie, he paused and looked at him. "Sorry for flying off the handle," he said. "It's been a tough day."

The men were treated as important customers, which did not go unnoticed by all who were in the bank. Mr. Everson walked them out to the sidewalk, shook each man's hand, then bade them goodbye.

Back inside, the teller remarked to him, "I guess that was an apology. Sort of."

Time had drifted past the noon hour on this day of heading toward the farm. The weather alternated between clouds and sunshine. Skinner's wagon led the procession, and there was much chatter and laughter.

"I'm getting hungry. When do we eat?" Claude asked.

"Let's get closer to home," Skinner called out. "Then we'll stop and wait for Harlen and the others to catch up with us. Is that okay with you, Utah?"

"Fine with me," he answered.

Tex broke into song. "Oh, that strawberry roan, Oh, that strawberry roan; went up in the east, came down in the west, still on my pony a doin' my best; oh, that strawberry roan." A stiff breeze dislodged the curls in his dark hair.

"Where do you learn all those songs?" Claude asked shaking his head.

"I grew up hearing them," was the reply.

The wagon wheels rolled noisily over rocks and silently through sand. Iron horseshoes nailed to hooves made noise when rocks were stepped on. Only the rattle of chains from the doubletrees could be heard when walking over the sand, and there were areas in the roadway - maybe fifty feet long - that were pure sand - referred to as a 'sand bed'.

Each grain of sand - some as old as time - had crumbled off part of a solid rock, either by rain, freezing and thawing, or even by the wind.

The men often glanced behind, hopeful of seeing Harlen, Price, and Mr. Baxter galloping toward them.

The day had started with sunshine and a warm breeze. By mid-afternoon the sun was mostly covered by clouds. The warm breeze of morning had turned up the humidity, and sweat dampened their clothing.

Dark clouds gathered on the horizon, and the warm breeze turned into a steady wind. Tree tops swayed back-and- forth and, at times, bent low.

"Looks like we might get rained on," Skinner said while eyeing the dark clouds. He gave the reins a shake, and the mules turned their walk to a trot.

They traveled down the tree-lined road in no particular order, and in time Claude positioned his horse close to Lucas and rode beside side him for a while. Lucas had remained wary of him since the persimmon incident but did not avoid him completely.

"This has been an interesting trip. Do you agree?" he asked Lucas.

"Yes. It has been. It's been real interesting."

After a few moments of silence, Lucas glanced at Claude who wore a slight frown and stared off into space. Events of the trip played in his thoughts, and he began to smile. The smile faded as hunger pains roamed through his stomach.

Claude broke the silence. "Tomorrow's my birthday," he confided. "I'll be fifty-two years old, and I don't have much to show for my fifty-two years here on earth. I've been thinking about going out to California." He paused, looked straight ahead trying to recall what he had done in those fifty-two years, and wondered why he had such little money to show for them. "I can pick fruit or work on one of those ranchos I've heard about. I've got a relative or two out there. They live in the valley, somewhere between San Francisco and Los Angeles."

Lucas was surprised that Claude would want to confide all this information in him. Not knowing what to say, he just nodded his head and listened.

Claude continued, "There's fruit trees and vegetables in that valley. There's plenty of water, and it's sunny and warm most all the time. Want to come with me?"

Lucas stared at him for a moment. "Noooo," he replied dragging out the word. "I've got family here. I can't go."

Several hours had passed and still there was no sign of Harlen, Price, or Mr. Baxter. Dark clouds continued to gather while lightning sent jagged forks across the horizon. Distant thunder was audible and growing louder.

"We better find a place to camp," Skinner said. "I'd like to find shelter of some kind. You men help me look."

The two Baxter boys rode up beside Skinner. "We're going on," one said. "We'll ride until it's too dark to see the road, then we'll stop for the night."

"All right," was Skinner's reply. "Be careful." The boys waved goodbye and put their mounts to a gallop.

Utah rode up to the wagon. "I ain't seen no creek," he said. "I'll be a dry camp, but it'll have to do. We got plenty of water and food."

Tex saw it first and said, "Look at that old barn over yonder. I don't see any other buildings. That barn is just settin' there in the field. Reckon we could get to it? I don't see no fence. Why don't we stop and some of us go take a look at it?"

Skinner drew back on the reins and the gentle mules stopped. "Whose property is it?" Skinner asked. "Anybody know?"

Everyone said, "No," or shook his head.

"I bet Harlen would know," Gramps said. "I don't know who owns the land or the barn, but I do know it's been empty for a few years. We don't mean to do no damage, and I think no one would care if we used it to get out of the weather."

Tex led the way with Gramps and Nolan following. Skinner and Wyatt stayed in the wagon, the rest stayed close and waited. The men rode around the barn looking to see how sturdy the building was for no one wanted it to fall down on top of them. Skinner climbed down from the wagon and walked to the barn and under the overhang. He stood, while judging its width, to see if the wagon could take shelter there.

Tex rode his horse to the opening of the loft and stopped. Tucking his legs under him and raising up, he placed his boots on the saddle. He stood tall enough to climb into the loft. Once inside, he was startled when a few birds took flight. There was loose hay and a few bales scattered here and there. The floor of the loft was clean, and he thought it would be a good place to lay down their bedrolls for the night. When each man was satisfied that the barn was safe, he raised his arms and motioned for the others to join him.

Two or three set about finding wood for a fire with which to cook supper. Utah arranged the wood the way he wanted it and prepared to cook their last meal over the open flame. He held up the empty coffee pot but dared not make coffee because no one liked the way he made it. He set it back down, hopeful that Price would soon arrive.

Skinner guided his mules under the overhang, making sure the wagon was sheltered. Then after a few more steps, they stopped. He walked between the animals to the front of the wagon and bent over to release the chains from the doubletrees.

He removed all leather strapping from their bodies - except their bridles - then led them out into the open. He rubbed, patted, and talked softly to them, then removed the bridles and turned them loose to graze until dark.

As the sky grew darker all horses were unsaddled but staked close to the barn, where they could eat the remaining green grass. Each man wiped down or curried his own horse, fed, and watered it. They stroked and patted the neck and talked to their faithful steed as if they were best of friends, for without a horse, a cowboy would be walking.

Finding a place at the side of the barn away from the wind, Utah built his fire. He took inventory of the food remaining since this would be the last evening meal. Setting aside the breakfast food, he brought the rest of the supplies to the fire and methodically placed them in pots, pans, and the ashes. The wind was still hot as it blew across their faces, and lightning crackled in the distance.

Gramps walked close to the road and sat down on a large rock. While Utah cooked supper, he watched for Harlen, Price, and Mr. Baxter to come into view. He himself was anxious for Price to hurry on in to make the coffee, for he was in need of some. He wiped sweat from his face but stopped, upon hearing hooves galloping a little farther up the road than he could see. He let out a yell when he recognized Old Don. He stood up and began waving his arms.

All three riders waved back, then stopped and dismounted when they came close to Gramps. "We're all at the barn," he spoke hurriedly and pointed in that direction. "Harlen, do you reckon it's all right for us to be there? We'll be out of the rain."

"It'll be all right, Gramps. Don't you worry. That property's been vacant for several years. You picked a good place to stop." All the while, they were walking toward the barn.

Utah greeted them holding the coffee pot out toward Price. "I filled it with water," he said.

Price laughed and said, "Hello, Utah," then measured out the grounds and set the pot over the coals.

By the time the food was cooked, Price's coffee had finished perking. All gathered round, holding out their plates and cups. "Eat up Men," Utah said. "I don't want to have to repack it."

There was little talk while they ate, but they kept a watchful eye on the sky, which was filled with dark rolling clouds. There was a constant roar of thunder, and not many seconds went by without lightning, which was now shooting toward the ground.

Harlen remembered a song he once heard and turned toward Tex. "Tex, I wonder if you know this song I don't know the name of it, but it goes like this: "Pretty little girl in the bottom of the well, doan cha know she's lonesome, wolves howling, howling all around; doan cha know she's lonesome?"

With a slight frown on his forehead, he replied, "I've never heard that song."

They could hear their horses' hooves stomping with every clap of thunder, as well as every streak of lightning. When they were finished eating, each man went to see about his own.

At that moment a loud clap of thunder startled Claude's horse, and he tried to back away pulling hard on the stake which held his bridle rein. Claude jumped up quickly and ran to grab the reins. When lightning struck a nearby tree, sending branches and leaves flying through the air, Blue began bucking and snorting. It was all Claude could do to hold on to the reins. His voice grew louder as he tried to calm him. The others led their horses into a stall, and bridle reins were tied to whatever was available.

"I've never seen Blue act like that!" Harlen said. He walked closer for a better look and also to see if he could be of help. "He's plain scared. Look at him. He's shaking."

"There's a lot of electricity in the air." Gramps said while rising to a standing position. He looked at the sky. "I'm afraid this storm is going to be a bad one."

Blue showed no signs of calming down as Claude held tightly to the reins. He bucked, snorted, fast-stepped and two-stepped, leading Claude away from the barn, across the road and into a grove of trees. The men watched helplessly, fearing any involvement on their part would only make matters worse.

Several large rocks - some nearly as tall as a man - were in the grove. Others stood in the open, outside the stand of trees. A few touched the trunks of large trees, as if there had been a struggle to see which one was to grow there.

When the wind rushed by, a cluster of wild flowers leaned first one way then the other.

On the ground inside the grove, moss grew at the base of a tree and had climbed a short way up the trunk. A few other trees had the green moss spreading around them. The largest patch of ground was bare of any vegetation but was covered with small gravel, except for one rather large flat top rock which seemed to keep watch over all the moss and all the gravel.

The thunder grew louder, and lightning cracked and sizzled, sending jagged shafts downward. Blue wanted to run away from the storm; the direction was immaterial. He reared up, pawing the air with his front legs, jerking Claude off balance. He stumbled and fell against the trunk of a tree just as lightning hit it, blowing the top half of the tree into the air. A current of electricity surged through Claude who held Blue's reins, sending the current through the reins and into Blue's body.

Both were thrown violently to the ground. They died instantly.

The jolt knocked Claude a few feet away from the tree and into the gravel. He lay looking at the sky, with mouth agape. Blue lay on his side. The nails which held the shoes on his hooves were pulled out, and the shoes blown off. They lay close by.

The rest of the tree fell back to the ground, it's limbs and leaves covering most of Blue.

The clouds drifted away to the east, still rumbling with an occasional flash of lightning. A few birds ventured out of hiding, singing their songs.

When the storm wore itself out and relative quiet returned, the men still at the barn began to stir around.

"I don't hear Claude, and I don't see anything moving in that direction," Price observed while looking toward the road.

"I bet Blue and Claude are half way to Viola by now," Harlen said with a chuckle.

"I want to go look at that tree that flew up in the air," Lucas said and walked in that direction. He stopped at the edge of the grove to let his eyes adjust to the heavy shade of the many leaves that still hung from the limbs on the trees.

Finally, he spotted a limb on the ground and walked toward it. The charred stump of the tree, which was still smoking, held his gaze until finally he turned to look at what was once the top of the tree.

Then he saw horse shoes and wondered why they were there. Stepping closer for a better view, he saw Blue's legs, and jerking his head around, he saw Claude lying close by.

Nausea welled up inside Lucas, and he half ran to the clearing.

"Harlen!" he called with a faint voice. "Harlen! Come here! Help! Help!"

They all hurried to see what might have startled Lucas.

They followed him, as he walked slowly toward the grizzly scene. He pointed toward Claude and Blue. In stunned silence, the men circled around those lying on the ground.

"God in Heaven …" was all that Gramps could say. He stood staring at Claude. After a few moments, he bent over and, using both hands, rubbed them down Claude's face closing his eyes. With his thumbs under the chin, he closed his mouth. Then he raised back up. "Look at his hair," he said.

"It's singed," Price said and looked at the burnt tips. "So are his eyebrows," he added.

"He doesn't have any eyelashes either," Gramps observed as he studied Claude's face.

Lucas looked away and his eyes studied a large rock. "Look at that rock," he said. "It's as tall as I am."

No one looked at the rock. All seemed to be mesmerized by the body of their fellow cowboy and the horse he rode.

Wyatt stayed behind Skinner who stood motionless, resting his hands on his hip bones. His short arms reached around his dad's waist, and his small hands held a handful of his dad's shirt. The normal pink on his chubby cheeks had drained away, leaving a pale color on his still-baby face. With wide eyes, he stared through the bend of his dad's arm at the dead man lying on the ground.

It began to sprinkle, and all realized Claude's body would have to be moved out of the rain. "I'll go get some rain gear so we can carry him up to the barn," Tex said and hurried back across the road.

Skinner and Wyatt went with him. They glanced over the saddles. Finding Claude's they pulled at the tarpaulin, dislodging his bedroll which fell to the ground. The men looked at each other. Then Tex said with a shrug of his shoulders, "I guess he won't be needing that."

"You want to stay in the wagon?" Skinner asked his son.

Wyatt nodded, climbed in, and sat down on the seat. His eyes followed his dad back across the road. He could no longer see him when they entered the grove of trees, and he blinked a few times, hiding the tears that had gathered in his eyes.

Tex spread the tarpaulin on the ground. All of them reached down, lifted Claude, and laid him on it.

"What about his boots?" Nolan asked. "They're good boots made of cow hide. Should we take them off? Can anyone use them?" he cast a glance at his fellow men. "It seems a shame to bury them in the ground."

"It's not like he's going to need them," Lucas observed. "He probably won't be up walking around."

They all looked at Lucas and smiled but did not laugh out loud.

"I know a family with a bunch of kids who sure could use them," Tex said.

Harlen bent down and lifted a foot. "Well, let's just pull them off." Tex bent down and helped him then took control of the boots. They rolled the tarp around Claude as best they could then carried him to the barn.

"Where shall we put him?" Nolan asked.

"Well......" several of the men murmured, and all looked around.

"We can't put him in the wagon because Skinner and Wyatt sleep in it," Harlen said. No one else offered a suggestion.

"Let's lay him right here on the ground and up against the wall," and nodded toward the wall under the overhang. And that's where they placed him.

Reluctant to leave the body of the man they had known for a long while, all of them either leaned against the wall or sat on the ground.

11

OUT OF THE STORM

The shadows of evening began to lengthen, stretching across the road. Rain had started once again, beating against the building.

Harlen broke the lengthy silence by voicing his thoughts outloud. "I was feeling pretty good about us getting the cattle to the sale barn without losing any, and I think the little dogies have found a good home. I'm pleased about that. But this... Aw damn." Shaking his head he looked back across the road. "Now we've lost a good man and a good horse."

"Utah, is there any coffee left?" Gramps asked. "I expect nobody's going to fall asleep right away."

"We've got plenty of coffee grounds," he replied.

Price stepped forward, "I'll make it." He lifted the pot out of the wagon and filled it with water. Grasping a hand full of grounds, he let them pour into the water from his closed fist.

Utah stirred the ashes left from the dinner fire and laid cross sections of timber across the embers.

Each man shifted to a more comfortable position on his little piece of dirt on which he sat while waiting for the water to boil. When it finished perking, Price lifted the large pot and poured its contents into waiting cups. Some sipped the hot coffee. Some blew into the cup to cool it. Still others gulped it down. They sat in silence for a while, trying to understand why all this had happened.

"Claude was a good horseman," Harlen said. "I don't know what else he could have done to calm Blue. But Blue was beyond calming down." He shook his head in bewilderment. The three-year old bay had heard thunder and seen lightning many times before. Why this storm upset him so, they would never know.

"Are we going to put pennies on his eyes?" Lucas asked. "I don't think he's going to open them. Why do they put pennies on the eyes of a dead man anyway?"

In the midst of their sorrow, the men laughed. "It's just an old custom." Gramps said. "I closed his eyes, and the last time I looked at him they were still closed."

"Why do people sit up all night with a corpse? It's not likely a dead person will be going anywhere." Lucas was full of curiosity. That brought on more laughter.

"Well, that, too, is an old custom, going back in time to our ancestors from the old country. When I was but a boy, one of our neighbors died. My grandpa and other neighbors sat up with him all night. Me and the rest of my family went over to pay our respects, and I saw pennies on his eyes. I was scared of the dead man and the pennies, - I don't know why," Gramps explained patiently.

Lucas made one more observation. "Claude rode beside me for a little while today. He said tomorrow was his fifty second birthday," he paused and lifted his cup to his lips. In the silence he continued. "I guess he spent all his money cause he said he didn't have much to show for his fifty-two years on earth. He said he was thinking about going to California."

Lucas called for a second cup of the fresh-made coffee that was Price's specialty.

"Claude woke up every morning in a sour mood," Nolan said. "It took two or three cups of the hot black stuff to start his day. I will miss him, but I won't miss some of his habits."

"He was a good worker," Harlen said. "He was a little different, but he was a good man."

"He liked to play jokes," Lucas said with a huff. "I busted his chops for one he pulled on me."

"Let's just leave him wrapped up, and tomorrow we'll put him in the wagon and take him back to the farm," Harlen said. "Skinner can make a casket and then we'll bury him."

"Where are we going to bury him?" Tex asked.

"I don't know for sure, but I expect in the Wyatt Cemetery. It's the closest."

The rain had slowed to a gentle mist, and Gramps and Nolan began to yawn.

The horses were quiet in their stalls, and a moon ascended in the sky, illuminating the field where the barn sat. No one looked across the road to the grove of trees in which Blue lay.

Wyatt had been asleep for over an hour when Skinner and Tex lifted him into the wagon. "I think I can get to sleep," Skinner said and climbed in beside Wyatt.

"Maybe we should all try to get some sleep. Tomorrow we'll be back at the farm," Harlen said, trying to stifle a yawn.

Skinner and Wyatt slept in the wagon bed as they had the entire time they had been away from home. Everyone else climbed into the loft.

Each man picked up his bedroll and sought his own place for the night. They scattered across the plank flooring, each looking for a place to lay his head, close his eyes, and just maybe, go to sleep. Gramps chose to be by a hay bale on which he could sit while pulling off his boots. Some chose to be near the opening into the loft.

Harlen moved his bedroll so he could see the meadow illuminated by the moon. In the distance, tree frogs called to one another. He was not sleepy and raised up on one elbow and, through the moonlight, looked into the distance wondering what his dad would say. What could he say?

Under the lean-to and on the ground wrapped in a tarpaulin, Clyde lay in his eternal sleep.

A light breeze blew against the barn, entering the loft through cracks and other openings. It whistled softly when the wind picked up. Sleep was a long time coming, as each man sought to understand why death had appeared so suddenly to claim one of their own - and his horse. The moon made its way across the sky, and the night wind blew gently through the trees. In time, the croaking of the frogs ceased and silence reined over the land.

Daylight found Utah stirring biscuit dough and Price pouring coffee grounds into the large pot. The camp fire blazed for a short time settling down into a bed of embers.

Soon everyone was up waiting for coffee, having led the horses out of their stalls and in to high grass. Conversation was slow getting started. Going home to the farm was on their minds. What to do with Claude was also on their minds.

They did not linger over breakfast nor laugh at what the day might hold.

After the wagon was repacked, making room for Claude's body and his saddle, they mounted up and headed home.

They reached Viola just before noon but continued on for another few miles before stopping to let the animals rest. Price used the last of the grounds to make coffee, and any food left from breakfast quickly disappeared.

Somewhere between Viola and the farm, they saw Joe, riding his mule in an easy trot. His long legs dangled down past the mule's stomach. He had heard the iron wheels long before he saw the horses or the wagon.

He remained in the saddle and raised a hand in greeting. "I was beginning to worry," he said.

His eyes swept over everyone and everything. Then he counted the riders and the horses.

"We seem to be short some men and horses. Where's your boys, John?" he asked.

"They got back yesterday."

Joe looked at Lucas.

"Lucas, your dad came to the farm looking for you. He wants you to go back home. You're needed there. I'll settle up with you in the morning," he said.

The young man nodded acceptance of the information. He had walked to the Haughn farm in early spring looking for a job. The men accepted him as part of the team. He pulled his weight in the fields and had matured some under the guidance of the older men. He and Price had hit it off the first few days, and Price sort of took him under his wing. He had learned much more the last few days.

Joe looked at Harlen. "Claude didn't make it back with you?" he asked.

"Well…yes, he did. He's in the wagon."

Joe looked at Skinner then at Wyatt. Without seeing Claude, his head turned back to Harlen.

He's dead," Harlen said in a quiet voice.

"Dead?" Joe's head jerked back. "How did that happen?"

"We camped last night at the old Winters' farm." Harlen began the explanation slowly and carefully. "We stayed in the barn which was across the road from that grove of trees. There was loud thunder and lightning, and Blue got spooked. Clyde could hardly hold onto the reins. Blue led him across the road and into the grove. The best we could figure is they got hit by lightning."

Joe's eyes, once again, swept over the horses. "They? "Where's Blue?"

"Lightning got him, too."

"Where's the saddle? And the bridle?"

Harlen wanted to laugh, yell, or scream at his dad's questions. He remembered what his brothers had said of their dad, that he was as tight with his money as the bark on a tree. Saddle? Bridle? Of course! Inventory items.

He calmly replied: "The saddle's in the wagon. The bridle's buried in Blue's hide."

Joe grunted and stared at Harlen.

By this time several of the men had dismounted and were standing close, listening to the conversation.

John Baxter remounted, and with bridle in hand said, "I'm going on home. So long Men. Harlen I'm much obliged to you."

He glanced at all of them, including Joe, then said again, "So long." His horse started home in a fast walk.

Joe swung down off Duke and walked to the wagon. He looked at the rolled-up tarpaulin but did not unwrap it.

"Well...that's a shame," he said. "He was a good man and a hard worker." Waving his hand back and forth, as if shooing away flies, he gave orders. "You men go on to the farm. I'll go to the cemetery and make arrangements. The Wyatt cemetery is the closest, I guess..." He paused to gather his thoughts, and after a moment he turned to Skinner.

"Find some good lumber and make a casket to fit this man's size," he instructed.

He walked across the road, each footstep stirring up dust. Grabbing the horn on his saddle and putting his boot in the stirrup, he mounted the animal. With a quick shake of the reins, Duke started back down the road in a gallop.

Joe's thoughts were on the cemetery, on land once owned by his grandfather, John J. Wyatt, now deceased. It was about a mile distant from the Wyatt house and close to the creek called Peggenroot. John had set aside the land for a public cemetery. The first person laid to rest there was his son fifteen-year-old Henry Clay Wyatt. Several graves had been dug since that burial, and Claude would be laid among them.

Joe remembered the story of the mercantile store and how it had survived the Civil War while sitting in front of the fireplace on cold winter evenings listening to his grandmother tell about closing the store and going back to Missouri. She said they thought they would be safer further north. She told about her three brothers who had taken up arms for the Union. Two were killed and one just disappeared and was never heard from again.

She paused a few minutes and rocked back and forth in her wicker rocking chair. She withdrew from her pocket a small handkerchief, trimmed with lace, and wiped her eyes. "Henry Clay was my only remaining brother," she said. Then she recalled that stormy December day in 1866 when he was in the store. A wood burning stove provided heat, and a keg was pulled up close for him to sit on. It was full of gun powder. Lightning came down the stove pipe and the keg exploded.

Duke trotted down the sunken road, past the cemetery, on his way to the house where the caretaker - grave digger lived. He knocked on the door and called out, "Bert, are you home?"

On the other side of the door, the wife of the caretaker brushed back her hair and tightened the belt around her house coat before opening it.

"We've both been sick for a week," she said in answer to Joe's questions. "A plague of some kind. Bert's hardly able to sit up. If you need a grave dug you'll have to get someone else."

Joe headed home and arrived just as Skinner drove the last nail in Claude's coffin.

He could see activity in the bunkhouse. Some men stood over an outside basin, splashing water on their faces to wash away the soap suds. Others stood in various stages of undress, looking forward to clean clothes.

Harlen was with his mother in the kitchen. In the absence of his dad, he handed her the money from the sale of the cattle.

"I'm glad you're home, Son. We were getting worried. It's just too bad about Claude."

Joe came into the room. "Gather up the men and meet me at the barn," he said to Harlen. Then noticing the money in Laura's hand, he reached out his own hand, and she gave all the bills to him. He left the kitchen and headed for the room which contained his desk. Harlen looked at his mother, but she only smiled at him. He left her there and went to gather the men.

The mules were still hitched to the wagon, and Skinner was standing by the finished casket. He and Harlen lifted it to the back of the wagon bed then shoved it farther in.

Then they climbed in the wagon and carefully lifted Claude and laid him in the freshly made casket unadorned of any padding or pillow. Skinner laid the cover over it, then nailed it shut.

"There's the casket and there's Claude," Skinner offered a smile and a few words of humor to ease the solemn moment.

Joe stood before the men holding the reins of Duke's bridle. "We're going to have to dig the grave ourselves," he explained to all of them. "Bert's sick. Let's get our shovels and go before it gets any later in the day."

Before mounting up, Skinner turned to Wyatt. "Run home, Son," he said.

The small house could be seen at the bottom of a steep hill on which trenches had been cut horizontally to divert rain water and slow erosion. Boards were laid across the cut for a bridge. Wyatt ran down the hill as fast as his young legs could carry him while laughing, hollering, and waving his arms.

He could see his mother standing on the portico of the small house waving her arms. He could hear her voice as she laughed and called his name.

On the way to the cemetery, the men talked among themselves. There were questions that needed answers. "Does Claude have a family around here? Does anyone know?" Several asked the same question.

"One time I heard him say that he had lived in Idaho," Nolan said. "He didn't mention a town or anybody, and I didn't ask questions. Looking back now, I probably should have. But I didn't."

Lucas joined the conversation. "He told me he had relatives in California. He didn't say where in California, except between San Francisco and Los Angeles, and he didn't say who his relatives were."

12

THROUGH THE
QUIET SPACES

They stood inside the cemetery wondering where to start digging. "There must be thirty headstones," Lucas said while pointing toward the neat short rows. "Why don't we just make one of them a little longer?"

Joe walked to the end of a row, placed his shovel in the ground, and shoved it deeper with his foot. "Skinner, come over here and measure the proper length and width and put a rock to mark where we'll know where to begin and stop," he said.

They all took turns digging and wiping off sweat with their handkerchiefs. The weather turned cooler by late afternoon, but no breeze reached down into the cavity of the earth as the digging neared six feet.

Nolan climbed out of the hole and stood looking around. "I don't like graveyards," he said to Price. "I was in one too many times during the Revolution. Too many graves to dig. Too many killed." He paused looking into the distance. "My whole family was killed, except one brother, when they started shooting." He turned his back to Price and said in a low voice, "He drowned a month later trying to cross the river."

"I think we're finished," Joe said and bent over to look at their handiwork. "I guess we can bury him now."

"Where's the preacher?" Gramps asked while looking around.

"He's not here," Joe answered. Then after a moment he said, "Gramps, you're good with words. You say something."

The sun was lowering, and the weather had turned still cooler. A gentle breeze blew through the quiet spaces between the headstones which had been placed with reverence at the grave of loved ones. In the distance mourning doves called to one another. The wind ruffled the men's shirt sleeves.

Harlen removed his hat, looked at the inside of it, then put it back on his head. Others stood perfectly still, looking either at the casket or into the dark bottom of the grave.

Gramps cleared his throat. After a few moments of searching for words, he began by calling upon God. "God, we return this man to you for his life here on earth is over. You knew everything about him before he was even born. As a baby, and as a young child, and as a man. We lived and worked together, but we know very little about him. You must need him for something else for his life was cut short so quick." Gramps paused for a few moments, and in the silence only the wind could be heard. As the sun lowered in the sky, tall trees surrounding the cemetery cast long shadows down the rows of headstones. Speaking again Gramps added, "I never heard him say Your name. But I never heard him say the Devil's name either. According to the words of Your Son Jesus, I trust he is in Paradise with you. Amen."

With ropes at each end, Joe and Price lowered the casket into the fresh dug grave. Then they picked up shovels and began replacing the dirt they had helped remove.

When that was finished, Price said, "We all ought to chip in and buy a headstone."

Joe had walked to the wagon and laid down the shovels. He turned to the men and said, "I'll buy the headstone. I'll go to town and buy one, have his name chiseled in it, and have it brought down and placed at his head. You don't need to chip in. He was working at the farm. It's my responsibility."

Harlen was amazed at the strict, stern, sometimes cranky, sometimes angry, sometimes yelling, man that was his father. He was surprised by his generosity since he was so tight-fisted with money. He often said to his children "If you can't pay cash for it you don't need it." But he was pleased that Claude would have a headstone.

Very few words were spoken on the way back to the farm as darkness gathered around them.

Nolan wondered if a family member would ever find the grave, or if anyone would stop and read the headstone, or if he would be lost forever. To him, cemeteries were lonely places.

Laura kept supper warm, and upon hearing them at the barn, she set the food and plates on the table. They ate quickly then went to the bunkhouse for all needed rest and sleep.

Harlen lay on his feather bed with his head resting on a feather pillow. Within minutes he was asleep.

Looking through the window at daylight, Harlen noticed the world had changed. No green grass and not even brown grass could be seen. Everything was covered in white. A cold front had moved in, bringing the first frost of the season.

After breakfast Joe called Lucas aside. He handed him his wages and thanked him for his work on the farm. "I've seen you on that stallion, and I've seen how you handle him." He fumbled in his shirt pocket for a piece of paper and gave it to Lucas. "I've wrote up a bill of sale, and I want you to have that horse. You can take Claude's saddle and a bridle from the barn. Now give me one dollar, and the horse is yours."

A happy smile crossed the young man's face, and the words "Thank you. Thank you" tumbled out of his mouth as he searched for a one-dollar bill among the money he was holding. Upon finding the correct denomination, he handed it to Joe and took the paper from his hand, folded it, and put it in his pocket. He hurried to the barn and led the stallion out of the stable. The men gathered around Lucas who was still smiling as he told them about the horse.

"Mr. Haughn gave me my horse - or actually sold it to me. I gave him one dollar, and he gave me the Bill of Sale. He said I could have Claude's saddle and a bridle from the barn."

They followed him to the bunkhouse where he gathered his few belongings. After a moment, he said good-bye and added he hoped to see them again. Then he rode away.

The former cowboys, field hands again, began to settle down once more, carrying out the chores that are required of farm life.

A few days later and after supper one evening, Joe asked Harlen to join him on the screened-in porch that was between the kitchen and the hallway. He sat in a straight-back chair, waiting for his dad to start the conversation. Tilting the straight -back chair onto its back legs, he stretched out his own. He could hear dishes rattling in the kitchen while his mother cleaned up after their nighttime meal. The sun lowered, then disappeared behind the trees in the orchard.

Joe leaned back in his chair, looked at Harlen, and said, "Tell me about your trip, the cattle, and Waymon Jenkins."

Harlen chuckled, then after a moment said, "The trip went okay until a pack of wolves jumped us. One of them tore the nose of one of the little dogies. We were on Clete Jonas' land, and he rode up to see what all the shootin' was about. I gave him all three dogies. I would have had to shoot the injured one, and I didn't want to do that."

Joe sat up straight in his chair. "You just gave away three dogies? You didn't get any money for them?" Harlen stared back at his dad. "I just gave them away," he said.

Joe turned his head toward the orchard and was silent for a while turning over in his mind, what Harlen had said. "Just gave them away! Got no money for them! Well, under the same circumstances I might have done the same thing, only I would have asked for a dollar or two. But what's done is done."

"How did you get along with Waymon?" he asked with a smile on his lips and a twinkle in his eye.

Harlen shook his head and said, "He's a peckerwood allright," and did not tell of the unpleasantness he encountered at the hands of the contrary little man. Then he added, "Isn't there another cattle buyer you could deal with?"

"No one this side of Kansas," he answered. "I guess we could put em' on the train and ship em' to Springfield. But then we'd have to ship from there to Kansas City."

Having retired for the evening, Laura was lying comfortably in the feather bed, listening to the wind. Tree branches creaked as the wind pushed them up, down, and sideways. Moonlight shining through the window lit up the bedroom, making shadows on the wall.

After a few moments Joe entered the room, undressed, and lay down beside her.

"Did you pay the bank?" she whispered.

He raised up and adjusted his pillow, taking his time in answering.

"I want to buy and sell more cattle, and I think we need to keep some money for our own use," he whispered back.

"But did you pay the bank?"

"No."

Laura watched the moving shadows and wondered how long it would be before the loan was paid off. For hours she lay wide awake, as one thought after another whirled around in her head.

In the late morning Laura was sweeping twigs off the front veranda. Joe was at the woodpile stacking fresh chopped wood. On a limb of a walnut tree that grew in the side yard, a jay bird was flapping her wings, jumping up and down,and piercing the air with loud scolding noises. Becoming annoyed at the screeching sound they both stopped what they were doing, looked up in the tree, and walked closer to see why the bird was making so much noise. Laura quickly lifted her arms into the air and gasped. "It's a snake!" Laura said loudly. "It's crawling to the nest. It'll eat the eggs or the babies. Whichever is in there. Joe, you've got to kill it before it gets to the nest!" He went inside the house and came back carrying a rifle. With the butt of the gun resting against his shoulder he fired. The bird was instantly frightened and flew to a higher limb. The long, fat snake fell to the ground. Unnerved Laura went in the house and Joe went back to stacking wood.

He was still at the woodpile when a horse dashed out from among the trees carrying one of his nephews. The animal stopped very close to him. He observed heavy breathing from the horse, noticed foam dripping from his mouth and saw that his body was covered with sweat.

"What's the big hurry," he asked with a frown on his face. "You trying to ride this horse into the ground?"

The rider, a full-grown young boy, dropped to the ground and spoke breathlessly. "Uncle Joe, I need thirty dollars so I can get gone before they arrest me."

"Arrest you? What for? What did you do?

"I was delivering moonshine to the boys in Viola. I was spotted but I ran away."

"You can't get any money from your folks, your dad?"

"Ma said to ask you."

"Well...I'm going to have to think about this."

"Uncle Joe there ain't no time to think. I've got to go now! Right now!" the young man pleaded.

Joe looked at him for a moment then lowered the axe to the ground leaning the handle on the stump. "Stay here while I go into the house and see what I can do."

Laura had looked through the window and saw them talking. Raising the window, she could hear the conversation. She followed Joe into his office and reminded him of the debt at the bank.

He counted out thirty dollars, picked up the bills, and frowned at Laura on his way out the door.

The young man was nervous, kept looking around and shifting from one foot to the other.

"Here's the money. Where will you go?"

He reached out to take the bills and shrugged.

"California maybe."

"Well…good luck, be careful, and leave your horse here. He's in no condition to run another mile. You can hitchhike and walk on your way to California."

The troubled young man left in a run. Joe went back in the house.

Laura knew how tight money was and fretted at Joe for handing out thirty dollars, which she knew very well, could have paid one month's payment to the bank.

He made no reply to anything she said. Instead, he went back to the woodpile and picked up the axe. Between his frustrations and Nolan's boredom, the woodpile was nearly as high as the waist line on a tall man.

"I'm not supposed to help out anyone on my side of the family?" he fumed outloud. "If it had been someone on her side, she'd been all for it." He was now chipping kindlin for the fireplace – bringing the axe down hard.

His anger was releasing its hold on him a bit and he swung the axe into the chopping block. Turning loose of the handle, he looked up at the sky. "Where on God's green earth is the money coming from?" he asked.

Harlen was in the barn loft pitching hay close to the opening in the front of the building when he saw a horse running through the trees and into the clearing. He recognized the animal as belonging to his cousin on his dad's side of the family. It seemed, by the swinging of the arms and the twisting of his body, that he had not come for a friendly visit. Harlen thought it best not to interrupt the conversation between them. He could see his dad was not happy as he stalked into the house and back across the yard to the wood pile, then hand something to his cousin.

He saw the horse's body heaving as he breathed and the foam dripping from his mouth, and he didn't like it. He didn't like to see animals mistreated, and this animal had been ridden almost to death.

He sat down and dangled his feet and legs through the opening in the loft, while he waited for the conversation to end so he could go to the horse and lead him to water. When his cousin left without the horse he jumped down to the ground and hurried to take hold of the reins.

His dad had walked down the road past the barn and toward the branch. The water was tipping the edge of its bank from the rain of yesterday. The roar of the rushing water could be heard from the house.

Harlen guessed his dad was angry and needed to be alone to calm down. He dared not go after him. Instead he picked up the reins, patted the neck of the roan gelding, talked to him, and led him to the pond. When the animal was in better condition he would take it back where it came from.

Gramps had ordered another box of cigars, and it arrived in the mail that frosty morning. He carried it to the bunk house, tore off the wrapping paper, then opened it. Picking up a slim, tightly-rolled cigar, he rolled it over and over with his fingers. Carrying a chair to the open door and holding the cigar close to his nose, he inhaled the sweet-smelling tobacco. He sat down, lit it and smoked it thoughtfully.

Harlen had not counted on his time being taken up by the cattle drive, and when he left, he did not put Star in a stable but let him run with the other animals in the barn lot while he was gone. He had already decided not to descend from the loft onto its back like he did other horses to break them to ride. This horse was different. It was one thing to get the buck out of an animal so a grown man used to riding could stay in the saddle, even with a little bucking. But Star was a child's horse, and he would use gentle ways.

In the early afternoon he walked across the barn lot carrying a bridle. He hoped to put it on the horse that had been brought to the farm from Missouri for him to break to the saddle. The owner's daughter had named him Star, after the patch of white on its forehead that resembled the shape of a star.

Star's body tensed, and he began backing up as Harlen approached. When he saw something in his hand, the horse raised his head high and pawed the ground. Stopping in front of him and making no effort to reach out Harlen spoke in a soft voice.

13

GENTLE WAYS

"Star, this is a bridle. It has a bit which fits in your mouth. The leather part fits over your head and behind your ears. Look at it and learn what it is. I'm going to put out my hand and touch your face."

Slowly he reached out, and Star backed up a few paces. He continued to hold out his arm while the animal showed some curiosity. Very cautiously Star took a step forward, stopped and stretched his neck to smell Harlen's hand. At the touch on his nose he drew back. He drew close again, and Harlen put out his hand and stroked his neck. He did not draw back.

Harlen left him then and walked to the barn. He hung the bridle on a peg in the tack room.

The next day he approached Star again, holding up the bridle for him to see. He tensed and backed a few steps.

Harlen whistled for Old Don who came running to his side. The ears on both animals shot forward as they looked at each other. The bit was put into Old Don's mouth, and the bridle fitted over his face and up over the ears. Then Harlen took the reins and walked him across the barn lot.

Star lifted his head and followed the man and his animal with his eyes but did not follow. Harlen led Old Don back across the lot and walked very close to Star without looking at him. Star turned to watch and took a few steps.

When they walked back toward Star, Harlen stopped and removed the bridle from Old Don and walked toward Star while holding up the bridle for him to see. He stopped and held out his hand. Star didn't move and Harlen fitted the bit in his mouth and slid the leather strap over his forehead and behind the ears.

He held the reins with one hand and placed his other hand on Old Don's neck and started walking. Star wasn't sure of what he was supposed to do and didn't move. Old Don walked a few steps while Harlen tugged on the bridle reins. "Come on Star," he said softly. "Let's go for a walk." Soon the animals were side by side with Harlen out front leading them across the barn lot then back and forth.

On this cold afternoon Price was on his knees on the bunkhouse floor, rubbing oil onto his saddle and shining up the silver pieces that were attached to all four corners. Nolan lay on his bed reading a book. Gramps held a pen in his hand, making circular motions with it as he wrote on thin white paper. He had friends and relatives in St. Louis, and he occasionally wrote to them.

In freezing weather, ice formed on top of the pond and had to be broken up so the animals could drink. Aside from breaking ice, pitching hay, and milking the cows, there wasn't much else for a man to do in the wintertime. If one was used to being busy, winter time was idle time which became restless time. And Gramps was used to being busy.

He approached Harlen one morning as they pitched hay to the horses.

"Harlen, I'm going up to St.Louis for a while. I've got folks up there. I'll come back in the Spring."

"Are you going to take the train from West Plains?"

"No. I'll thumb a ride. It won't take long to get there."

Gramps laid his clothes in the suitcase and put the box of cigars on top of a shirt, then put the lid down and locked it. Then he picked it up and walked out the door. It was a mile to the main highway where cars went whizzing by.

Harlen asked Price if he was going or staying, and his answer was simply, "Next year."

Nolan had no place to go and managed to keep busy chopping wood or cleaning out the stables.

Star had been on the farm three weeks and had become familiar with the other stock in the barn lot. There were horses, cows, calves, chickens, cats, kittens, and a couple of dogs. Occasionally a hog and her piglets were let into the lot for the safety of the young pigs. Laura had half a dozen geese brought in to keep Crabby company. For the most part, they all got along as they went about their daily lives. They walked and ran together, and it seemed Star and Old Don had become best friends.

Star was used to Harlen's soft voice and let him rub and pat him, put a blanket and saddle on his back, and even a few times let him climb up and sit in the saddle.

Joe spent a great deal of time chopping wood in the rather large area where logs were piled up. Between him and Nolan, there was enough fire wood to last several seasons.

Joe seemed vague each time Harlen asked how much acreage he wanted plowed and planted when spring came once again. He didn't press him for answers. He figured in time they would come.

Joe was getting worried. A letter had come from the bank reminding him of his outstanding loan. He wondered where the money would come from to even make an installment on the principal-and that didn't include the interest. At that moment, he wasn't even sure they would have the farm when springtime came.

Harlen mentioned to his mother that his dad seemed distracted or worried about something, and he wondered if she knew why. She looked away and said, "Oh. He has a lot on his mind." Then she would smile quickly and change the subject.

From the kitchen window there was a clear view of the barn lot. Oft times Harlen could be seen riding Star who responded to every command. He had a smooth gait, and Harlen once remarked to his mother, "Riding Star is sort of like sitting in a swing." Old Don showed signs of jealously and followed their movement with his eyes.

Harlen felt confident that Star could safely be ridden by the little girl. He wondered when they would come to get him.

Before he could see the vehicle, he could hear the roar of the engine. Then, on this bright sunny day with all the snow melted and a little warmth in the air, Joe had joined Harlen in the barn lot to talk about buying more cattle. They turned to see a truck pull up close to the barn. A man and a woman got out of the cab, shut the door, and start walking toward them.

At first, Harlen didn't know who was approaching and went to meet them. He recognized the man but not the woman who stood beside him.

"We came to get Star." The man said.

"He's my horse," the woman stated.

The man stuck out his hand for a gripping handshake which Harlen acknowledged, as did his dad.

"I'm Theodore Lankston from Missouri. I brought the horse to you to gentle for my daughter to ride. Is he broke to the saddle?"

Harlen was confused expecting to see a child.

Seeing the confusion on his face, Mr. Lankston introduced his daughter. "This is my daughter Memry Lankston. Memry, this is Harlen Haughn and Mr. Haughn."

Joe only nodded to her.

"Happy to meet you, I'm sure," Harlen said, staring into her eyes and shifting his feet nervously.

"I'm delighted to meet you," she responded.

He stared at the young woman with brown hair, hazel eyes and a friendly smile on the prettiest face he had seen in a long time. She held out her hand while Harlen struggled to remove his gloves to acknowledge her greeting. The touch of her small, soft hand sent chills down his back as she squeezed his in a handshake.

"Can I ride Star? He won't buck me off?" she asked him.

"Su-su-sure you can ride him. He's pretty gentle." he stammered. "I'll go get him." He turned and walked toward the barn. She followed. They walked across the barn lot toward the animal. Star watched them approach then started toward them.

"Star!" she called out, and he trotted to her. Old Don saw them approaching, and he, too, started toward them.

"Let's go to the tack room and saddle both of them. We can ride across the lot. I don't think Star will buck you off."

He saddled both and led them out in the open. Adjusting the length of the stirrups, he helped her climb into the saddle.

Star stood perfectly still.

They walked the animals at first, then urged them into a trot. Harlen couldn't help casting glances at her as she rode by his side.

A neighbor girl who he had walked with to a dance on several occasions crossed his mind. She was a good dancer and so was he. After the dance he walked her home.

Then there was the other girl who laughed at anything – refusing to take life seriously. They met occasionally in the cedar grove. Any cares he had seemed far away when he was with her.

But this young woman who rode by his side and put her small hand in his - by way of a handshake – and met his glance head on had shaken his composure.

After a short while, he rode Old Don to the gate. He leaned down and opened it, and they went galloping across the field toward the creek. The horses waded into the water, lowered their heads, and drank their fill.

Memry laughed easily while telling Harlen about the purchase of Star.

"He wouldn't let just anybody ride him. He would buck them off. I told my dad I wanted him to buy Star for me. After much persuasion, he finally agreed, but he wouldn't let me try and ride him. We heard about you and brought him down here."

"I wouldn't let him buck me off," Harlen said with a laugh. "I jumped off a couple of times. He learned quick what was expected of him. He and my horse, Old Don, became good friends."

They rode back to the barn where Joe, Memry's father, and the truck waited. Mr. Lankston handed a five-dollar bill to Harlen who reached out to take it then put it in his pocket.

He unsaddled Star and exchanged bridles. Then the animal was led into a stall which was padded with soft leather to prevent injuries to any animal that was being transported. He and Memry talked.

"Where do you live?"

"West Plains."

There was a roar in his head, not from the engine of the truck, but from the way she looked at him. All other noises, except her voice, were blocked out. He could smell a fragrance about her, like roses that bloomed in springtime beyond the gate on the way to his mother's garden. It made him a little light headed. "I'd like to see you again," he said over the roar of the engine and the one in his head. "I'd like to see how Star is progressing. I get up to West Plains now and then."

"I would like that," she said. "We live just outside the city limits, on the south side. Our farm says Lankston Stables. You cn't miss it." She reached out and touched his arm. "Thanks for training Star so I can ride him." She observed his slim face and small nose and mouth. She studied his eyes. "When you come to West Plains, please look me up. I would be very happy to see you."

She walked with her dad back to the truck and climbed into the cab. Then the truck drove away from the farm.

The men standing in the barn lot watched the truck as it made its way to the highway. Old Don raised his head high and nickered. He and Harlen watched until it was out of sight.

Price walked up to Harlen. "Looks like Old Don has lost his best friend. And with that mooney-eyed look on your face, it looks like you just gained a best friend.

"Are you referring to the young lady who looked like a million dollars with a split skirt, high top boots, and a hat on top of her head?"

"Yes. I am. The young lady with that same mooney-eyed look on her face," he teased. Then turning thoughtful he said in a low voice, "Mr. Lankston has to have a sizeable bank account to pay for that truck. He could very well be worth that much money." They both stood looking up the road, the same direction the truck had gone. "I guess you'll be going up to West Plains now and again?"

Harlen smiled but did not give an answer. With the bridle reins in his hand he led Old Don back toward the barn. He was thinking about Memry when he became aware of an annoying sound and turned his head in that direction.

Crabby, with wings spread, neck arched and an open beak was screeching and running in circles. Harlen stared as the gander ran toward him, bit down pulling on his pant leg then bit him just above the knee.

"Ouch, Crabby," he said and rubbed his leg. "What's the matter with you? Have you gone crazy?" Old Don lowered his head and snorted causing the gander to run away. "Run you crazy old thing. We could have gander soup you know." He and Old Don continued toward the barn.

With lowered wings Crabby calmly walked back into the group of geese and started pecking at insects and a few scattered grains of corn that had escaped notice of any animal.

"You better behave and stay with your own kind," Harlen shouted. "My mother wouldn't want anything bad to happen to you."

THE END

CPSIA information can be obtained
at www.ICGtesting.com
Printed in the USA
LVHW021523230920
666823LV00005B/235